GET A GRIP

A SHORT STORY COLLECTION

KATHY FLANN

Texas Review Press
Huntsville, Texas

FIRST EDITION

Requests for permission to acknowledge material from this work should be
sent to:

Permissions
Texas Review Press
English Department
Sam Houston State University
Huntsville, TX 77341-2146

Previously published stories in *Get a Grip*:
"Neuropathy," *Carve*
"Half a Brother," *Michigan Quarterly Review*
"Little Big Show," *Chattahoochee Review*
"Get a Grip," *New Delta Review*
"Homecoming," *Blackbird*
"Leaving Reno," *Southern Humanities Review*
"Show of Force," *Blackbird*
"Heaven's Door," *West Branch*

Cover Design: Nancy Parsons, Graphic Design Group
Cover Photograph: Howard Yang
Author Photograph: Howard Yang

Library of Congress Cataloging-in-Publication Data

Flann, Kathy, 1969- author.
  [Short stories. Selections]
  Get a grip / Kathy Flann. -- Edition: first.
     pages cm
  ISBN 978-1-68003-051-8 (pbk. : alk. paper)
  1. Baltimore County (Md.)--Fiction. I. Title.
  PS3606.L359A6 2015
  813'.6--dc23
                                                  2015018056

ACKNOWLEDGEMENTS

A number of people read early drafts and helped to make these stories better—Matt Ellsworth, James Magruder, Jane Delury, Christine Grillo, Jen Michalski, David Ebenbach, Glen Retief, Julianna Baggott, Bill U'Ren, Betsy Boyd, Tim Train, Michelle Tokarczyk, and Matthew Hale. In addition, Ron Tanner and Anna Schachner helped to make meaningful revisions to nearly-final drafts. Len Small, graphic designer and friend, provided guidance and vision for the front cover. Special thanks to Elizabeth Spires and Madison Smartt Bell for encouragement, help, and sage advice.

Although it has been a while since they were my mentors, I hear their voices when I write or teach —Judy Troy, Fred Chappell, Michael Parker, Lee Zacharias, and Jim Clark.

Goucher College offered generous support for this book in the form of grants and a sabbatical. The Virginia Center for the Creative Arts provided invaluable time, space, and fellowship. The Baltimore Office of Promotion & the Arts and the Maryland State Arts Council provided grant support.

Thanks for the encouragement of my family— Mom, Dad, Kate, Stephanie, Zac, Rachelle. I'd like to acknowledge the family members I lost while writing this book—Homer and Clark. Finally, I want to thank my husband, Howard, for his insight and his steady kindness.

"My mother had a great deal of trouble with me, but I think she enjoyed it."—Mark Twain. This book is dedicated, with love, to my mother.

CONTENTS

GET A GRIP

A Short Story Collection

NEUROPATHY

You scan The Shopping Network again for the thing God wants you to buy, the thing for the troops. Those barely-shaving boys. There are wind chimes, brooches, stop-snoring aids, mini trampolines. And more stuff of no value to young men in Humvees, young men storming rooftops, shooting at cars, frisking villagers whose kind brown faces are costumes. Your bad hand clutches the remote, zapping the volume, daring your fingers to do more than throb in concert with your boring heart.

The presenter, Petunia, offers the profligate items in a baby voice. She jokes about wrinkles she doesn't have. Words line up in your throat like fighter jets— something like, "Get more Botox! Maybe it'll paralyze that mouth!" You clamp them inside your lips, the hot of engines. Fool outbursts at the television aren't Christ-like. And they could make the hand flare up, the pain an electrical storm up your arm. Which you maybe deserve. But according to your smarty-pants son, you also risk a blackout, and the last thing you need is him down here lecturing you again.

The next product she presents is the American flag—not something the troops need sent. Still, an icy-hot pool seeps in your stomach. You lean forward and squint at Old Glory. It's shiny. Like maybe it's fashioned from the same stuff as a rain slicker. Utility impresses you. If you were made of something like that, maybe you'd have endured the winter better —your husband dying in that shameful way and everyone around here knowing about it.

Her porcelain hands flutter along the flag's contours as she rattles off its dimensions. "Everything about this flag is standard military issue," she says, "except for one thing." The camera pulls close and she takes a bite out of the corner where the stars are. She chews and smiles. "Delicious," she says.

You gasp, bring your good hand to your mouth.

"That's right, folks." She dabs at her pink lips with a napkin. "One hundred percent fruit jerky." Your scalp tingles. The daily inspiration card you drew this morning featured Proverbs 20:13—*Do not love sleep or you will grow poor; stay awake and you will have food to spare.* Food! Can this possibly be a coincidence?

Ever since Wayne died, you crave a calling, a flourishing endeavor, like the ones church friends have—Monique gathers restaurant breath mints for women's shelters, Pat takes old people to The Golden Corral on meatloaf night, and Ken fills out tax returns for the needy. You have tried some things that fizzled, like a used medical equipment bazaar and a clothing drive for big & tall homeless men.

But then God showed you. A junkie you'd given a dollar staggered off the harbor wall. Dropped. Disappeared under the brackish film. His matted hair drifted on the surface like seaweed. You watched, frozen. It seemed like a long time before that soldier in fatigues brushed past and sprang from the edge. He lugged the incoherent, babbling man, shoved him onto the retaining wall. The soldier, freckled baby-face all red, climbed out and hurried away, trailing water. Didn't even give his name. This was *it*. Could anyone be more inspiring, more filled with the holy spirit, than a warrior, someone who tamed death?

You go to the wall calendar, circle the Fourth of July. You'll be able to airmail these babies to Afghanistan by then, no problem. Your bad hand shakes such that you can hardly dial. But for a rare moment, you forget the ache, the throb. It's like zero gravity, like you could float out the window and sail over Baltimore, could drift to the Middle East in this bathrobe, coasting on warm air currents.

"You ordered what?" says Peyton, who has just gotten out of bed, even though it's 3 p.m. Your son works graveyard shifts at Hopkins as a patient care tech—what used to be called an *orderly*. "Soldiers can't *eat* the American flag. That would be desecration."

"Desa-what?" you say. "Talk English." You know what the word means; you're just irritated how he uses it against you.

Peyton sighs in that way he has. There's been a certain tone ever since he started studying for his nursing degree at the community college.

He hulks in the doorway, filling it like an eclipse. The weight of his gaze turns your head toward the window, toward the coneflowers so pink against your strip of manicured grass and the May sky. So pink against the two meth-heads meandering down the back alley, both clad in gray T-shirts and dirty jeans. People like that are exactly why, after the accident, you stayed home and raised your boy instead of finding work you could do one-handed. Wayne made just enough managing the Royal Farms convenience mart. It had always given you a thrill, the fact that your husband was employed. You return to folding Peyton's boxer shorts, still warm from the dryer, holding them under your chin to fold, and placing them in the laundry basket. He wears all of these strange European labels now, and the fabrics are slippery as eels. Even the good hand can hardly hold on.

Those boys in the alley—they're just a few years older than he is, nephews of people you know. He could have turned out like them, like so many from this neighborhood, this gray labyrinth of formstone —wandering and wandering, with gaunt faces and protruding teeth like skeletons, like ghosts. It's not as if you'd prefer that.

Peyton smirks. You can feel it, but don't turn your head to look. "Wouldn't it make more sense for soldiers to eat their enemies' flags?"

"Muslims have a flag?" you say. You're sure they don't. But it seems to make Peyton so happy when he's smarter than you. You go into the kitchen to pour him a coffee in a Johns Hopkins Hospital mug—the cupboard is full of the things. And he keeps bringing more home, like maybe the hospital will disappear one day and he'll need a souvenir.

He is laughing. Now he stands in the kitchen doorway. He has a habit of following you around the house, your shadow. He accepts the mug of coffee and blows on it.

Then he lowers himself onto a kitchen chair. He's only twenty-one years old, but the chair looks too small. He spills over the sides. You rummage for the Coffee-Mate and the sugar, and he waves them away. You keep forgetting that he takes it black now. Bad enough that he's been lifting weights since he was thirteen. But he's also persnickety about what he eats and drinks. Says his body is a *machine.* "Of course, you do understand the whole concept of *enemies* is problematic?" he says.

You raise a skeptical eyebrow. You won't say what you really think—that enemies are real and they are everywhere. There's our weak mortal flesh. That's obvious. But there are other things that lurk, like Daylight Savings Time—things that seem benign until something happens the way it did with Wayne.

"I understand a lot of things," you finally say.

You wonder if this is true. When you ordered

the flags from the nice lady on the phone, what you pictured was Peyton and you sitting at this kitchen table late at night filling out airmail labels together, just the way the two of you used to sit here and work on his science projects. Right now, you understand you may have been wrong about the probability of such a thing happening.

"Is it bad today?" he says, nodding toward your hand.

You shake your head and shrug off his question so that he won't drone on about neuropathy, about how it's a sleepy, garbled conversation between your hand and your spinal cord and your brain, about how drugs would make it better.

"The flags are full-sized," you say hopefully. "You know—like a regular flag." The steady throb is like the drip, drip of water, something that could drive a POW insane. You glance at Peyton while you wipe the countertop, and you consider switching the sponge into the bad hand so that the pulsation might explode to white hot, to a light you might see when you shut your eyes. Maybe it could wipe the slate clean, the way a mortar shell does.

He stares into the mug.

"And they come in a pouch," you tell him, your voice brighter, steadier, now that you have imagined a purge. "Like those ponchos we got at the Ravens game that time?"

Peyton was only sixteen then, and you used the last of your savings to buy him those tickets for his birthday. Wayne didn't come—what with his work schedule, the extra shifts, the meetings with staff. But you and Peyton had fun in those purple get-ups, talking and having snacks, even after it was clear the Ravens would lose and even though the temperature dropped to thirty-five. Wayne called Peyton a *mama's boy* that night, and flashed his trademark grin, the one with the cute overlapping front teeth. Peyton opened his math book wider and gave Wayne the finger. The way they loved each other *was* boyish. Your two boys.

"The flags are grape-flavored," you tell Peyton. "Like Fruit Roll-Ups."

"*Freedom* Fruit Roll-Ups?" he says. "You still have those weird dolls from last month out in the hallway."

You don't see what was so bad about those dolls. The company had taken black celebrities and made them white with blond hair and blue eyes—white Dionne Warwick, white Sidney Poitier, white Nat King Cole, white Kobe Bryant. They had also made white celebrities black. The black Marilyn Monroe was especially pretty.

"They're called *Reverse Racism* dolls—"

"It's cute."

"It's *not* cute," he tells you. He runs a hand through his hair.

Last month, he refused to load the dolls into the SUV to take them to the city schools. And he physically blocked you when you tried to do it. "Maybe I can change those black kids' lives," you told him. "Maybe they can—"

"Can what? Lighten up?"

"No," you said blinking at him out there in the dark. "Maybe they can see that looks don't matter. Maybe *this* is the key!"

He lifted the box out of your arms. His voice softened. "It isn't, Mom," he said. At the time, you'd thought maybe God was using Peyton to communicate with you. But you probably shouldn't let Peyton stop you this time. If Jesus had had a grown son, maybe that son wouldn't have approved of him, either. Would that have slowed Jesus down? Would he have kept his miracles in stacks of cardboard boxes in the foyer?

Peyton drains the last of his coffee and clinks the mug into the sink. "You do know that God doesn't watch The Shopping Network or care which crap you buy."

"God is everywhere, Peyton."

"Was he in Pop?"

You close your eyes. So long as no one mentions Wayne out loud, you're able to keep the bad parts at bay. Now your synapses itch and you can't stop it. Normally, if you keep the TV on, the memory doesn't replay over and over and over.

You sigh. "I can't speak about your father's relationship with God," you tell your son. "Only my own."

Peyton shakes his head. "That pastor at the funeral couldn't do it, either."

You had no way of knowing that by the time a good Samaritan called at 8 a.m., Wayne had already been carted away, had already succumbed to the cocaine-induced heart attack he'd had in his neon SUV parked on 36th. It is the neighborhood's main drag, its shopping district with Paradise Uniforms, David's Consignment Furniture and Pawn, and of course, Dmitri's Tavern, which, on that day, like always, had opened at 6 a.m. It's a place where the firefighters go after their night shifts, a place where a person can grab a beer to take outside and keep him warm at the bus stop or on a bench.

You smile and fold your arms as if this whole conversation with Peyton has been playful. You pretend it has been. You pretend you don't worry about Wayne's soul, about whether you'll see him again when your time comes.

If it had all happened one day earlier, Daylight Savings Time would still have been in effect. It would have been dark at that hour and people might not have noticed the girl running down the street, her blouse open. She would have escaped the scene, remained anonymous, the way she wanted to. The Dmitri's Tavern crowd would not have gathered around her or around Wayne's Blazer. The good Samaritan would not have called and you would not have hurried the few blocks down there to be greeted by gasps and giggles. You would not have had to endure their descriptions of him in the driver's seat, the way his eyes were open, the way his jeans were pushed down past his hips, the way his penis was still erect. "Better you hear it from us," they insisted.

You would not have seen all of those hands pointing at the girl on a bench across the street, the girl you recognized as a Royal Farms employee, her knees pulled up to her chest, head hidden, friends gathered, trying to comfort her.

If it had been one day earlier, dark and quiet, probably a policeman would have knocked on your door to deliver the news, leaving out most of the details. Your husband wouldn't now be any more of a stranger than husbands normally are.

"Go take your shower and I'll make you some eggs," you say to Peyton. You can do most things one-handed. It was something Wayne admired. He kept one of this own hands behind his back sometimes to see what it was like. He'd admired the way you wore your ring, even though the constriction of the metal was unbearable. And when the finger finally swelled too much, he took it, and he wore it on his pinkie, right next to his own. Peyton has the rings now, retrieved from the undertaker, tucked away somewhere in his tidy room. That's your boy.

"No eggs," he says. "I'm meeting Suzanne at the mall."

Unfortunately, Peyton also has his late father's Chevy Blazer—the unmistakable thing is emblazoned with lime green ads that a local radio station paid Wayne to have painted on there. You're not sure which is worse, that you have to ride in what everyone now calls the "pecker-mobile" or that you're stranded in the neighborhood when Peyton goes to work. Or to the mall. You don't drive, of course, because of the hand. Your husband crashed into a tree years ago—the protective arm he thrust out no match for the gravitational pull toward the windshield.

You smile and shake your head, as if this might make it seem like you're delighted Peyton's leaving for the mall, not hurt. You had imagined that this day, the day you ordered the flags, was special—the two of you might celebrate.

"You and Suzanne never get to ride anyplace together. Shame." His friend is in a wheelchair. She used to be a patient at his work. The city's handicapped bus, which requires appointments three days in advance, is how she gets around.

He shrugs. "It's too hard for her to maneuver into the Blazer. The seat's too high and the ceiling's too low."

You remind yourself that he's being a good boy. Maybe he takes after you! You've been paying twenty dollars a month to the Christian Children's Fund for the past thirty years. The Navajo boy you sponsored at the beginning has already grown up, robbed a gas station, and gone to prison. Sometimes he writes you the most beautiful letters, full of quotations from scripture. He's Catholic, but his heart's in the right place, so you still mail him the twenty dollars, even though he's too old for the program.

"Ma?" Peyton says, his voice soft. He starts to put a hand on your shoulder, but then pulls away, like maybe he'll hurt you. "I will *not* drive you to mail those flags overseas. Return them, okay? It's too much money."

You nod.

Maybe he'd see things differently if you could share your news about the $150,000. The man from the bank said that Wayne had won that money from the Maryland Lottery *years ago*. And confound it if he hadn't put every cent in a trust for you and then kept living the same way, as if the winning ticket had never happened. You should have told Peyton by now, but every time you open your mouth to say it, your eyes well up, your throat goes dry. Maybe you, too, want to keep living like it never happened.

Your boy doesn't hug you on his way out. He doesn't rest his chin on your head. He doesn't say, "You're the best." They are all things Wayne used to do before he left for work. He had done them that final morning, a morning with the sun searing through the living room blinds an hour earlier than the day before.

The following week, the UPS man delivers the fourteen cases of edible flags on his hand truck. Peyton wanders into the living room, trying to find you amid the towering stacks. "Hey Ma?" He peers over a box.

"Mm-hmm?" You're crouched, opening one with some splayed scissors. The hand has taken to shaking more lately. Probably he'll be too focused on getting rid of the flags to notice. *Here we go*, you think.

"Ma?"

"*What?*" You look up.

"I asked Suzanne to get married and whatever." He clears his throat. "And she said okay."

You haven't yet met Suzanne, but you have pictured someone with withered arms and legs, someone who can't speak clearly or hold her head up. You hadn't known he would consider dating such a person, let alone marrying her. "Oh," you say. "I see."

"I'm serious," he says.

"I understand that."

"She wants to meet you."

"Well, I mean, how can you . . . *know* that for sure?"

"What?"

"I suppose you've found a way to communicate with her?"

"Ma, she's not like Stephen Hawking," he says laughing.

"Who?"

"Cut that out!" he says, laughing harder. He

wags a finger at you. "I'm onto that. You know who Stephen Hawking is."

You grin. When was the last time you had this kind of fun together? His face is different—you see the child he used to be, the slightly lop-sided smile and the brown eyes that close almost completely when he's happy, like the Buddha statue on your hippie neighbor's stoop.

He composes himself. "Suzanne was in a car wreck. Just like you." He gestures to your hand, the one that shattered to dust after Wayne swerved across the center line. Wayne said there'd been a dog in the road—something you question now, after the way he died. That car accident had been the end of your career as a flower arranger, one of the best in the shop. "Just think if your spine had broken instead," Peyton says. "That's Suzanne."

"Oh," you say. It's the most he's told you about his life for months. "Well, congratulations." You hug him and he lets you. His hands light on your back, and you hold on. Your fingers throb into the ridges of his spine.

The next day, when you return from distributing leaflets for the church bake sale, Peyton stands next to a tiny blond girl in a wheelchair in the living room. The flags are stacked in the front hall with the dolls. He keeps insisting they go back, and you keep making excuses.

The girl is as beautiful as a TV star, with platinum hair that looks like it has been in hot rollers and a spray of freckles across her nose. If not for the chair, maybe she would be out of Peyton's league. The boy's big, sure, but he still has some acne and he hasn't really grown into his nose and, as far as you know, he's never really had a girlfriend before. You'd been like that at fifteen, when Peyton's father had sauntered up—on foot—to the drive-through window where you worked and retrieved a strawberry milkshake he hadn't even ordered. No one had ever asked for your phone number before.

An icy vacuum opens in your stomach. Maybe she wants Peyton for that money. In your logical mind, you know you're the only one who knows about it. But still. The feeling prickles your skin like frost crystals.

"I'm going to run out for pizza and let you two get acquainted," Peyton says. And he leaves. Just like that.

She appears to be resting, like she might at any moment jump up to fetch her compact or a diet soda. Maybe she is like a faking villain on a soap opera.

"Will you need help using the ladies room?" you say, talking louder than normal, stepping forward. It occurs to you that maybe she has a power to make people feel sorry, to make them do things, just like Wayne did. He'd had a promising football career dashed by a bad elbow in high school, and he'd finagled prescription pills from sympathetic doctors ever since. You always thought he needed them.

Suzanne laughs. "I'm good."

"Because I'm stronger than I may look," you say, making a muscle.

"Peyton told me about your terrible accident."

You blush. What has he said about you? You have been a mother who spent years in darkened rooms, afraid to fill pain pill prescriptions because of your husband. Maybe he'd steal them. Or worse yet, maybe they'd be as wonderful as they seemed when your husband's eyes shrank and dilated away into something more blissful than you'd ever known. It scared you how much you wanted to go to that place with him. Better to endure the crush and pulsation of your hand—the pain like something alive, like company.

You can still see your boy's pudgy, babyish twelve-year-old face staring at your hand the first day he rode his bike over to visit you in the rehab hospital, his father probably in a bar somewhere dealing with a different kind of pain. Maybe it was guilt about the accident, some need for swagger, for bravado, that led him to the cocaine he hid until the day he died.

The young Peyton regarded your newly un-bandaged hand with horror, yes, but also fascination. "It looks like it's made of putty," he'd said. And then a dawning realization registered on his face. "You won't send notes with my lunch anymore."

"Maybe I can learn to write with my other hand."

He'd burst into tears. "But it won't be like they're from you."

Without thinking, you'd reached over to wipe his eye. It hurt and you flinched, and then he'd cried harder.

You've been lucky to have a gentle son. If he were inclined, all he'd have to do is squeeze, and he could reduce you to animal agony. There are women on this block whose sons have hit them—police dragging flailing and shouting young men out to cruisers late at night.

"So, Mrs. Polasky," Suzanne says now. "Those are the edible flags in the hallway?"

Your cheeks warm, like she's caught you in your undergarments. More things he's been telling her about you. You clear your throat. "I want to send them to the troops, but Peyton thinks—"

"He worries too much!" she says. "He thinks about every decision for a month. It's a wonder he can decide what to wear."

"He proposed to you. That was a big decision."

"He kept chickening out," she says with a shrug. "He kept taking me out for fancy dinners and ordering champagne and stuttering." She begins to imitate him in a goofy low voice. "Uh, um, Suzanne, uh, um. It's just, well, um." She laughs.

You cannot picture the person she's describing. Your stomach burns with a feeling you can't identify.

"Peyton may be hard to read, especially with knowing him such a short time."

Suzanne laughs again. "I don't think so," she says. "I love the guy, but one thing I know I'm not signing up for here—and that's a life full of surprises."

Heat rises in your throat. You imagine moving behind her and grabbing the handles on the chair and pushing it out the front door. But you feel guilty for even picturing what might happen next—the careening down the front steps, the toppling onto cement.

So you imagine instead walking out the front door yourself. You would slam it behind you. You'd wander around the neighborhood like those meth-heads do, slipping off the main avenue and down back alleys. Looking at the rowhouses from the back, at the long skinny rectangles of grass, at the dilapidated home-built balconies, at the abandoned children's toys, at the pairs of shoes in neat lines—it would seem like an invasion of the most intimate kind. You'd peer into everyone else's lives the way they'd peered into yours, crowded around that SUV.

But you do not move toward the door; you do not disappear, only to return when the sun burns pink at the horizon. You have never been full of those kinds of surprises. Maybe that was why Wayne sought solace elsewhere. You close your eyes. Then you go to the kitchen.

You bring Suzanne a glass of ice water. She sips it, looks at you brightly. "Why don't you take the flags to the VA hospital instead? It's so close."

It takes eternity for Peyton to come back with the pizza—Suzanne chatters about whether the Red Men's Hall or the Republican Club would make a better wedding venue, whether Triscuits or Ritz are better for the ham and cheese appetizers. "Uh-huh," you say. You can't stop thinking about her idea, its perfection, the likelihood that in that lightning-flash moment that she said it, she was an empty vessel filled with God. For you.

Even after you're all eating at the table, you only half pay attention to the two of them as they talk with their mouths full, discussing how great the disabled van has gotten lately, always on time, never getting lost like it used to.

You wonder if that soldier who dove into the water was actually a veteran, maybe in uniform because he'd gotten home that very day. Maybe *veterans* are God's real mission for you. Your heart buzzes in your chest like a little engine. The VA hospital is just off Fayette Street, right? You'll get there somehow, independent and resolute like that soldier, like you're on a mission. And hey. Maybe Peyton will see that you like people in wheelchairs as much as he does, no matter how objectionable they may be.

On your way to the bathroom, you spy Suzanne's sparkly black purse on the floor, some of its contents spilling out. You scoop the lipstick and the barrette back inside, and then you study her ID card for the handicapped bus, the fetching photo. When you slip the ID into your cardigan pocket, you don't know why. It's just that you have to—the Bible card you drew this morning was Isaiah 6:8 *And I heard the voice of the Lord saying, "Whom shall I send, and who will go for us?" Then I said, "Here am I! Send me."* Sometimes, humility is about getting out of His way. Jesus was nothing if not resourceful.

You step out of the handicapped van, and you arrive at the front desk of the VA, clutching one case of flags. The woman sitting there doesn't even look up from her *People* magazine. "Donations over there." She points in the most lazy way possible toward boxes and bags at the opposite end of the lobby—a mountain of them.

You clear your throat.

The woman finally glances up. You flash her Suzanne's ID photo. You hold it out, close to the woman's face. "My daughter-in-law," you say. Maybe another reason you have this card is so that association with someone pretty will get you better service. "She helped me gather these items." It isn't true, of course, and you try not to think about the panicked way she and Peyton searched the living room the other night or about that moment when she hung up the phone and said, her eyes brimming, that it would take six weeks to get a new ID from the city. "I have to *prove* I'm disabled," she said, reaching up for Peyton's hand. "What does that even mean?" You refused to look out the window while they tried, for half an hour and without success, to maneuver her into the Blazer without contorting her back in painful ways. Finally Suzanne's mother had to drive in from Harford County with her large van. After they were gone, Peyton grabbed three of his Hopkins mugs and smashed them on the sidewalk out front. He swept up the shards before he went to work.

The woman at the VA studies the ID for a moment and then stares at you. What she sees, you figure, is a skinny lady clutching a too-big box to her too-apparent bones. She blinks. Will Suzanne's beauty compensate for your lack of it?

You smile in a way that you hope is Christian enough to keep your stuff out of that landfill across the room. Then, you pat the cardboard with your bad hand. Too hard. It tingles. You stifle a flinch, shut your eyes. "Everything in this box is brand new." Earlier, at home, you stuffed some of the dolls in there, too. "*This*," you tell the woman, "is a special box."

The woman smiles and winks, like she's sending a message and you'll understand it. Wayne used to wink like that before he went out at night, not to return until 4 a.m.—the wink like code for something private and special. Maybe an acknowledgement of the child you reared for him, the home you kept. But you're not as adept as you thought with codes.

The woman comes around the counter, and you step back, unsure what she'll do to you. She hoists the box onto her shoulder. "I'll put it right on my boss's desk."

This is more like it.

A few days later, the director of the VA phones to say what a hit the flags are with the veterans. Some of them have apparently been weeping while they eat them. "Wait, what did you say?" You give your full attention to the voice on the phone.

"It's very cathartic for men with post-traumatic stress." He pauses. "Oh. And those dolls. They're certainly strange. But they fostered a fascinating conversation in group therapy."

His words begin to take shape in your brain. "That's wonderful!" you say. "I mean, well, I don't mean it's wonderful. But you know what I mean."

He laughs and it is gentle, kind. "Would you like to come meet the men?"

A knot blossoms in your throat where the word *yes* should be. You picture the way the soldier hustled into the crowds of tourists, disappeared. Maybe sensing your hesitation, the VA director says, "*The Sun* wants do a story on this."

"I'm not looking for attention," you tell him. It feels good to say this, to let go of earthly concerns. But you do imagine the pastor holding up the article for the congregation—the headline something about a local hero.

"I get it," he says. "So much shame." He lets out a disapproving sigh. "You *and* your daughter."

He means Suzanne? You swallow a lump. Maybe you're in trouble for the ID. Or maybe, you think brightly, he has you confused with someone else.

"Two in one family. What very brave ladies." He

sniffs, takes a deep breath, like he marvels at his own words. "You are such an inspiration. From now on, when I have trouble getting out of bed, I'm going to think of you."

Your brow furrows. Mouth moves. Wait, *what*?

"Let's not hide you two under a bushel." He says he has arranged an initial meeting with the reporter and the photographer for tomorrow. "Mrs. Polasky, will you please wear short sleeves like you did the other day?" he says. "So we can see your affliction?" He pauses. "You might as well be proud of what God has made you. That's what I tell my guys."

Comprehension snaps like a mousetrap, pins you in place. Your lungs deflate, dead flaps in your chest. He wants a photo spread of you, Suzanne, and the vets—everyone broken, in need of repair. Maybe pull on the heartstrings of donors. A last puff of air escapes. You see yourself the way he does: You're not the soldier. You're that junkie in the water, spluttering, green snot oozing down your lip.

You slam the receiver down as if you are hitting the man's face, which is probably clean shaven and probably sprouts from a starched collar and tie. "Ugh!" you yell, slamming the receiver three more times. Maybe you even hold it in your bad hand on purpose.

"What the hell, Ma?" Peyton calls. His feet rumble down the stairs.

"Cripples!" you yell out. It feels good to say such an ugly word, like splashing into icy water.

Peyton appears in the doorway. "Ma, you can't do this."

You try to wave a finger, but they have curled in a new way, like a claw. "God punished Suzanne, Peyton." You spit when you talk. "How did she make God angry?"

"I don't believe in God," Peyton says. For a moment, you are too disappointed he isn't angry to hear what he's saying. You want to yell at someone.

You sputter for a moment, words not finding any traction. "Well then what do you think has become of your *father*?"

He shrugs. "It's like you think he was an actual person." Peyton steps closer, tiptoeing. He lowers his voice. "Look around this place. Wayne didn't pick out a single thing. He was never here. And did you even notice? He sold your jewelry."

"That's not true." You study the shelf of photos of Peyton, the lace curtains, the India ink drawings of football players that you gave Wayne for your first anniversary. Your mind scans back for the last time you saw your ring on Wayne's finger. "You have our rings in your room."

"Where did you get that idea?"

Your pinky tingles, cold—gentle at first as if it's asleep. But then the nerve endings harden all the way up your arm, not warm white lights, popping and fizzing, the way you imagined. There are just your own ordinary eyelids, dark and unsparing, like amputation. You want to yell out. Maybe the vibrations in your throat could crack you back apart, the way noises could start avalanches, covering something, revealing something. Your vision narrows to a long tunnel the shape of the nerve. You are lying on the carpet.

You can hear Peyton hover over you. "Ma?" he says. You open your eyes to see his brow furrow. He reaches for something on the floor beside you. Then he inspects it.

It is, of course, Suzanne's ID, which has fallen out of your pocket. "Why the hell do you have this?" Ah, *now* he decides to get angry—now that you can barely make a sound. He has one hand up. Maybe he's going to slap you. You almost wish he would.

"I have her ID," you whisper, "because I need it more." You're sure this isn't true. And that's how you know what you've done is as bad as things Wayne did. Your behavior has been garbled, like a conversation between three people who can't hear each other. You extend your bad hand. You offer it to Peyton. Maybe he'll take it, crush it, send you into permanent sleep.

And then, in a move quick as a wrestler, he picks you up. He carries you up the stairs. On the bed, you open your eyes, and he leans in. He flashes an expired bottle of OxyContin from Wayne's bathroom drawer. "You're going to take these goddamn pills," he says. His eyes well up. He clamps his lips, as if he can trap his sadness inside. And you understand that this moment, right now, is why he works out, why he studies—so he can care for you. But all you can think about is what Wayne maybe already knew, that it hurts not to be punished. Like a dry heave or a hollow tooth socket, or the last cocaine slicked along the gums.

You open your mouth to let Peyton put the pill on your tongue. The sleep is deeper than you've ever had—so deep that waking is a fast elevator ride. You gasp twelve hours later when you open your eyes.

In the morning, you step over Peyton, asleep on the floor next to your bed, curled on his side. You take half a pill, and you pay a neighbor boy to load the SUV with every box in the front hall, dolls and flags alike. You drive for the first time in years, crawling along at twenty miles per hour. The lurching, heavy foot on the brake pops your neck. Cars honk. You have forgotten to adjust the mirrors. Vehicles on cross streets roar by in confusing, divergent streams.

New condos, glass and modern, have appeared where a Save-a-Lot used to be. A man with two prosthetic legs walks the intersection of Erdman and Edison, way out toward Dundalk, washing windshields for money like he has always done. A breeze ruffles your hair. You hold the wheel with both hands and there is no throb. No good or bad. The hands are silent as friendship. The only occasional sound inside the car, one that you don't know when you last heard, is your laugh.

It's only a few miles to Crazy Ray's junkyard, but it takes an hour to dump the pecker-mobile. Then another two to get back via the bus.

Peyton sits on the front stoop in his pajama bottoms and a Hopkins T-shirt. He doesn't ask about the Blazer, almost like he has been waiting for the past six months for you to drive it to the dump. Soon, Wayne will buy his son a fully loaded handicapped accessible van—as if he was an actual person, as if that was the way God made him.

It is still early. "You're awake," you say.

HALF A BROTHER

Valdur—with his impossible wingspan—reached into the taxi, all the way across the passenger seat, and placed his hand on the Russian cabbie's shoulder.

"Don't!" I said. The traffic light had just turned green. "If he drives away, you'll break your arm." Behind my brother, I bent down and waved. Maybe I could defuse the situation with my vaguely Russian looks. I was boyish and gangly, not yet shaving daily like Valdur. But the cabbie only directed wide angry eyes at me, his jaw muscles tensing like he had marbles under his skin. The cars behind the taxi honked.

"Come on, man, give us a ride," Valdur said, in his even, sunny tone. He always sounded the same, whether he was talking to our former social worker, Allison, or he was celebrating yet another of his personal bests for the Druid Park High School Legends basketball team. He had a voice like a man with a yacht, a man with no worries except for deciding how many hours to nap in the sun. "We have money," Valdur told the cabbie, revealing the wad of bills in his other hand, money our mother had given us from the cash register of Karu International Food Mart, which she owned.

The cabbie responded the way all cabbies, store

clerks, and restaurateurs responded to us, regardless of shoulder manhandling or Russian-ness—he pretended to be busy. He flipped on the "occupied" light and punched the gas, the engine roaring in a startling burst. And then he became a tiny toy cab on the horizon, or at least on the horizon of Liberty Heights Avenue and the Baltimore sky, the shrinking sound of his music, the only evidence he'd been here.

Valdur, who had withdrawn his hand at the last second, lost his balance and now sat in the road, smiling. He shrugged. "I tried," he said. I reached down to help him up, all seven feet of him, before he got run over. He was the only person I'd ever known who was taller than my own six feet and nine inches. And we were both still growing. I figured I might catch him because, even though our mother had started us in school the same year, he was ten and a half months older. Every night, I sneaked into the kitchen and polished off whatever milk was in the carton, and I ate my mother's verivorst, her blood sausage. I thought tall thoughts.

Valdur bent over and brushed the road dust off of the dress slacks we had special ordered from Niedermyer Big & Tall; they'd arrived yesterday, just in time, and they had cost a whole month of wages. Our mother had pinched and juggled the books so that she could pay us in advance for our usual job stocking shelves in the food mart in the evenings, after practice. Normally, we wore shorts or the Druid Park High track pants that Coach had gotten us after he realized we didn't own pants. Now, Valdur licked his finger and rubbed at a dusty smear on his thigh. "Stupid as a table leg," I told him, over the hum of traffic. "We can't get picked up by the police before we even make it to the interview."

"Well what's your idea, Malev?" he said, gesturing in an exasperated way toward the broken down number eighty-three MTA bus that still sat down the block.

"This town isn't that big."

"Yeah, but we are," said Valdur. "And nobody's going to stop for us."

"You go and hide behind that dumpster. Maybe they'll stop if there's only one of us."

"Why me? Why not you?"

A knot blossomed in my throat. "Well, it's just . . ." I gestured to my own face and then I gestured to his.

Valdur's jaw went slack as if I'd punched him in the gut. It was the closest I'd ever come to saying that I was the one who could pass for white, while Valdur looked vaguely like a giant Dominican, with coffee-colored skin and soft curly hair that drifted away from his head as if he were in zero gravity. The truth was that we didn't know what we were. Our Estonian mother, blond and blue-eyed and six feet tall herself, wouldn't tell us. Whenever we asked who our father was, she only laughed and shrugged and said, "Old Nick," which was Estonian for "Santa Claus." Then she would push her reading glasses down and study us over the top of them, her pen hovering in the air over an inventory list. "It doesn't matter." Then she would do her imitation of *The Godfather.* "Capisce?"

Now, we stared at each other for a moment, nearly nose to nose if I stretched, and I could see Valdur calculating his options, the yellow flecks in his brown eyes like electric sparks. He closed them for a second and sighed. I was sorry about what I'd said, but we didn't have enough time to mess around. Loyola's coach had told our high school coach that the higher ups didn't know why they should "take a gamble" on a couple guys who'd only stepped on the court for the first time a year before, a couple of guys still learning the differences between street ball and real ball, a couple of guys with C averages at one of the worst schools in the city. With his hook shot and his magic at the free throw line, someone would take Valdur if Loyola didn't—but what about me? I'd fouled out of three games in front of college scouts.

Now, Valdur turned and walked behind the dumpster, which only came up to his stomach, and he flipped the open metal lid down, disturbing a cloud of flies. He waved them away, studying my face all the while in the same bloodless way as he looked at opponents on the court. I had never been on the receiving end of that stare, and strangely enough, my feet began to tingle. Finally, he crouched down. Why had I said what I said? Maybe I wanted him to know I had a shot with that white girl at school that we both liked—Carlene Carnegie from the hip-hop dance squad. She was tall like a supermodel and had a tattoo of the Irish flag on the top of her breast.

There was a long pause.

"I ain't no garbage man," said his voice, finally, from behind the dumpster, and then there was another silence. A *garbage man* was a player who did the dirty work on the court.

"Yeah, bitch?" I muttered. "Look at yourself."

I wondered if he'd heard me and then he said, in a cartoonish voice, "Hellooo, garbage man." He started giggling. And suddenly we were both laughing. I had to bend down to catch my breath. Just like that, we were brothers again, a matched set regardless of what we looked like.

In Estonian, matched sets, like arms and legs, could only be referred to in the singular. If you wanted to talk about one hand, you had to say "half a hand." That's how we were—like hands attached to the same body. Everyone, even that writer from *The Baltimore Sun,* called us "The Eastern Bloc."

Just like I'd predicted, after a few minutes, a cab slowed down for me. It was a lady cabbie—an older woman in a denim vest whose biceps were nearly as big as Valdur's forearms. She didn't turn her head to look me over, but just sat idling, waiting for me to get in. Right away, I could smell the herring in the rosolje that sat next to her in a Tupperware container, and I couldn't believe it. A whole bunch of

Estonians had come to the US at the same time as my mother, after the collapse of the Soviet Union, and Baltimore certainly had its share—just not usually in our neighborhood. I knew our luck had changed. But I also knew that if she did turn to look at me, she'd see a big blue-eyed guy with jet black moppish hair, someone who could be mistaken, by an Estonian anyway, for a Russian, if a tan-skinned one—and that would *not* go down well with said Estonian. So I made a preemptive move. I opened the rear door, leaned down and said, "Kas sa saaksid mind aidata, Prova?" *Can you help me, Ma'am?*

Now the lady whipped her head around, and she actually clutched at the head rest on the passenger seat, and pulled herself one hundred and eighty degrees where she sat, even with her seat belt still on. She had the same heavy lidded eyes, fair skin, and full lips as my mother, but she had light brown hair and sharper, more bird-like features. She grinned and her eyes sparkled with mischief. "Paras pähkel," she said. *Quite a nut.* Which was an expression that meant, *Tough question.* Ah, sarcasm. We were used to that.

"Come on, come on," she said in Estonian. "I'll take you wherever you want."

Her eyes grew large, as people's often did, when she first clocked Valdur. He peered over the dumpster, and then got taller and taller and taller as he straightened his legs. He nodded at me, grudgingly, and then emerged, taking his long careless strides toward the car. He was only eighteen, but he had the square form of a man and the stubble of a full beard; he wasn't a beanpole like me. He folded himself into the backseat of the cab beside where I already sat. We each had to put our feet in the other's floor well, our limbs tangled together, our knees strained against the vinyl backs of the seats. "Vabandust, Prova," I said, since I was the one who sat directly behind her.

"No need to apologize," she said. "An Estonian

is like a tree." She put the car into drive and pulled away from the curb. "Now where are we going?"

I explained that we were on our way to our academic interview at Loyola. Valdur told her how we were running late, how we had to hurry to get there on time. The coach had arranged this meeting. He believed that if the provost of the college laid eyes on us, experienced our impeccable manners, heard about our lives firsthand, he would finally grant the Athletics Department one extra scholarship so that we could both come, and not just Valdur. Valdur had also been offered scholarships at a couple small schools on the Eastern Shore, but none of them were Division One.

"Wait, wait," said the lady. "I know about you. Someone told me. They said there are two Estonian brothers who just started playing basketball for the first time a few months ago."

"A year ago," said Valdur.

She turned her head to study us for a moment. "You don't look like any Estonians I ever saw. Or any brothers I ever saw."

Neither of us knew how to respond, so we were quiet for a moment. People in our neighborhood pretended not to notice our appearances, and it felt like the time someone had stolen the only towel I owned out of my gym locker and left it out on the bench—like an intrusion of the most intimate kind. Sure we didn't look exactly alike, but was it so noteworthy? Was this how people outside of the world we knew would talk to us—as an odd couple? Were they right? She seemed to sense the awkwardness in the air. "But I am making an elephant out of a gnat," she said. "What matters is that now you are stars."

"It was hard for the coaches to convince our mother to let us play," said Valdur, seemingly as happy as I was to change the subject.

"She wanted us to keep working in her shop after school," I added.

"Where there's work, there's bread," said the lady, laughing. These were exactly—exactly—the words our mother had said to Coach Brewer, except she'd said them in English. Her lips had been pursed and she had refused to look up from her own work as she spoke. The Coach had brought his whole crew to the food mart—the assistant coaches and the physical trainers—to show Mother how serious he was about recruiting us to the Druid Park High School varsity squad. They stood behind her in a row, baseball caps in their hands. It wasn't until Coach mentioned the possibility of college scholarships that she lowered her pricing gun, placed the sült down in the refrigerator case with the rest of the meats, and turned toward him, one blond eyebrow rising like a door creaking open. She flipped a stray strand of hair with the back of her wrist. "Being big as a horse," she said, "can actually earn you money?" Up to that point, feeding and clothing us had been a military operation. We had sidestepped involvement in gun-dealing and drug-dealing, which was how some kids in our neighborhood got by, mainly because the toughest guys wanted us for show—to hang at their parties or walk their kids to school. But they never said why. It was kind of the code where we were from that the more different someone was, the more you should act like you didn't notice. We were the elephants in the room.

If not for Mr. Kim, our downstairs neighbor, having that crush on Mother, leaving her the food mart in his will, we would still have been on public assistance. Allison would still have been our official social worker, someone to help mother navigate the maze of services, instead of a friend who stopped by to say hello each week. And even with the food mart, Valdur and I could literally eat half her profits if we didn't qualify for free lunches. So mother's pragmatic side edged out her post-Soviet mistrust of institutions —Coach Brewer's offer for us to join the high school team meant we not only had the prospect of college money in the future, but we also would get snacks and Gatorade at basketball practice.

"Listen," said the lady cabbie now. "My name is Oie. I'm going to get you there on time. Don't worry." *Oie* meant "wind." It seemed like a good omen. I sat back and let the breeze ruffle my hair. I turned toward Valdur, and he smiled his genuine smile for the first time all day—a dimple on one cheek and his eyes crinkled to half their normal size, just the same as they had since he was spindly-legged kid with missing front teeth. I put my fist up and he tapped it with his own. Then he palmed my head with his expansive hand, and for a long moment, we sat like that—his hand on my head—not saying anything, just feeling the warm wind blow from the window.

Since we had found out about the scholarship possibilities and realized that this might be real, we might go to college, we might not spend our lives working with Mother at the food mart the way we had expected—well, we had both become quieter. Normally, we used to lie in our twin beds at night giving each other shit about Carlene Carnegie or miming free throw techniques and critiquing each other or hatching a plan to catch that one Asian shoplifter who kept coming in the back door. But now we both stared at the ceiling night after night listening to each other breathe. Then finally the other night, Valdur had said, "Don't laugh. I mean it." I had turned on my side, the springs squeaking beneath me. The moonlight shone through the small attic window, and I could see his eyes, wide open, looking at the ceiling. He glanced over at me for a second—a piercing look that said he meant it. I shouldn't laugh. Then he looked back at the ceiling. "If the NBA doesn't work out—"

"Don't worry. College will shape us up. Coach says—"

"But if it doesn't," he said. "What will your major be?"

"What's a major again?"

"You know, the subject you want to study. So you can get a certain job."

"When we retire from the NBA, we could be announcers," I said, lifting up onto my elbow.

There was a long pause then. "I think maybe I could be a teacher."

I did have to stifle the urge to laugh. A teacher? Valdur? That would be like, like being an Eskimo or a cowboy or whatever—it seemed like something you just were, not like something you could become. But he had turned on his side to face me, and I knew that this was serious. "Why not?" I said. "Sure."

It was the first time it had ever occurred to me that our lives might go in different directions, that I might not be the first consideration in Valdur's choices. Allison had been jabbering away for years about our futures, even bringing us brochures for Baltimore City Community College, making sloppy heart-shaped loops around the tuition assistance information with that purple pen of hers. But she had never told us that in this college version of the future, each of us—Mother, Valdur, and I—would live apart from each other, would be alone. I had lain awake most of the night, long after Valdur's soft snores had begun to waft into the attic eaves, like insulation, cushioning the room.

Now the cab passed by Druid Lake, with its low wrought iron gate. It was not yet nine in the morning, and scores of bicyclists, mostly African American, some Latino, some white, cruised the path around the water—not all of the bikes from the Bikeshare program had been stolen. A lot of these people were from our neighborhood, and stopped by the food mart for bottles of water. In the summertime, you had to go early because there weren't any trees around the lake, no shelter from the searing light of the sun, just huge expanses of impossibly green grass. "There's Cassandra," I said pointing out the window. "And

Dion. And Frank." We had very rarely been farther away from our neighborhood than this lake, especially since we'd grown big, and as it retreated behind us, we both craned our heads to watch it disappear.

The last time we had ventured away a few months earlier, it had been to the Inner Harbor. Mother had finally relented and said we could celebrate the regional championships on our own. We hadn't been allowed to go to the pizza parlor in Towson with the rest of the team because she had decided it was too far away. "Back before dark!" she had said, narrowing her eyes so we'd know she meant it.

We had walked the brick pier along the deserted waterfront, the March sky hollow and gray, the Hard Rock Café sign and the red Phillip's Seafood sign bright against it, chocolate ice cream cones in our hands. We were so engrossed in reliving Valdur's second-half three-pointer that we were late to notice the policeman confronting us. He was small, overweight, and he muscled up to Valdur, poking him in the chest. "What's that in your pocket, son?"

"Cell phone," Valdur said in that even voice of his, giving a little shrug. He hadn't shown his sticky palms, hadn't stepped backward again and again, dropping his ice cream and nearly tumbling off the edge into the water. His eyes didn't go wide, the way that men like this seemed to crave from Valdur. In fact, Valdur responded the way he always did—which was not to respond at all. He hadn't even stopped walking, which forced the policeman to scamper along side, like a nipping dog. When Valdur put his hand up to block the man from poking him again, that was, apparently, the last straw. We hadn't even been wearing the Colorado Rockies hats of the Crips or the Cincinnati Reds hats of the Bloods. Our heads had been bare, for anyone to see. But nevertheless, we found ourselves in the Harbor Police Station waiting for our mother. This would not have been a good predicament for any high school boy, but for us it was especially bad—our mother didn't have a car because she couldn't afford one and because she didn't like to leave the neighborhood. She hadn't left, in fact, for a couple years.

Allison drove her to the station and waited outside. When our mother appeared in the lobby, she was a new shade of pale, even more so than the day that we came home from an exceptionally intense practice and Valdur fainted in the Laotian aisle. "The people, the police in our neighborhood know you," she had scolded, sputtering in Estonian. Then she pointed to some distant point outside the window. "Out there, every boy idiot wants to pick a fight with the biggest, the most splendid." She rarely expressed her admiration for us, and we both blushed, though Valdur's complexion made it harder to see. Technically, *he* was the biggest and, by virtue of his scoring record, the most splendid. So it took me by surprise for any number of reasons when Mother turned to *me* and collapsed in my arms, her eyes moist, her face buried in my chest. I had never seen her show emotion like this before. Maybe this was what she'd been like as a pregnant nineteen-year-old immigrant, someone with no job and no English, someone whose family had issued strict orders to land an American husband and had disowned her when she failed. She reached out a hand and put it on Valdur, though she didn't look at him. "We keep him close," is what I think she said then, her voice muffled in my shirt.

And right now, in the cab, it hit me—that she perpetually grieved for us, but especially for Valdur, for the things the world would do to him one day. She was the only other person, besides me, who understood that Valdur's size and looks and temperament made him a living bullseye when he was outside our neighborhood. Even Valdur didn't understand that he was as vulnerable as any fluffy fresh-hatched chick—one that we could not cup in our hands. She looked up at me that day, and it had been as if our eyes were talking. When the scholarship offers had come in for Valdur, those other schools on the Eastern Shore—we hadn't even considered trying to wrangle me onto those teams, even though it would have been easier. Sure, it was partly that Loyola was Division One. But also, how could we go such a cruel distance from Mother? Loyola seemed cruel enough.

"I know the shortest way," said Oie, the cabbie, and soon we were on I-83 heading north. Within minutes, the warehouses and the billboards for Ram's Head Live and Canton Fitness Club gave way to thick green forest.

"Where are we?" said Valdur

"This is still the city," said Oie. "Loyola is in the city."

She got off a few exits later, and we wound our way past a nursery with rows and rows of shrubs and dogwoods with their roots in burlap sacks, past a playground larger than the block we lived on, past a row of fancy restaurants nestled in woods and gazebos, past some houses that looked nearly as large as our school. We were only twenty minutes from home, but it was like we were on safari.

"What do you think, boys?" said Oie.

"I don't know," said Valdur. "I can't see anything past all of these trees."

Charles Street, the road that led to the college, was no different. If anything, there were even more trees, bigger ones. They lined the street and towered over the car. "There is Notre Dame," said Oie. "And there is Loyola. They're right next to each other."

We peered out the windows. Squinting past the foliage, we could just make out large stone buildings, sort of like the English manor homes we'd seen in those boring PBS detective programs Mother liked to watch. Oie turned down the winding main drive for Loyola, but after a quarter mile, we discovered the gate down; a uniformed security guard emerged from the little stone building there and waved the car away. "We're on lockdown," he said. "You can't come in here right now."

Oie turned around and then idled near the main road for a moment. "What shall we do, boys?"

Our own school was pretty much perpetually on lockdown. Every time someone set off the metal detector with a little .22 or an X-acto knife, we had to stay in our classrooms for fifteen minutes until they cleared the person from the lobby. It happened so often, they rarely even suspended the offender anymore.

Valdur and I high fived each other. "Lockdown. Ha, good," I said. "Maybe they won't be too angry if we're a minute late." Oie telephoned a friend who worked as a housekeeper at the college. I looked at my watch again—seven minutes until the interview. I felt as though there was a pile of rocks in my stomach.

When she got off the phone, Oie said, "She says you can get to your building on foot. Just over there." She pointed to a stone path on the other side of the driveway.

"Kui palju see makseb?" I asked.

"Don't be silly. I won't take your money," said Oie, waving her hand.

"Tänan väga!" said Valdur

"Pole viga," said Oie. *No problem.* Then she waved out the window at us as we ran toward the path. "Kivi kotti!" she said. *A stone in the bag.* We would need her good luck wishes if we were going to make it on time. But what luck we had already had! Valdur blew her a kiss, and she tucked her chin into her neck and blushed. I knew that he was doing that as an excuse to do exactly what I was doing—to study the side of the cab and memorize the name and number of the company. We would mail her some money later. One day, on SportsCenter, we would make this woman famous when we told our story.

For now we charged into the darkness of the

woods, the air suddenly cooler, and almost wet. We could hear nothing except for the slight rustling of the leaves overhead and the sounds of our dress shoes on the stones and the huffing of our breath. Full court press. We'd make it! We were going to make it! I felt myself smiling, and I looked over at Valdur, and he started to laugh, like *Can you believe this?* His cloud of wavy hair bounced, and he grinned like after that first time he dunked during a game, a wide unselfconscious grin that would be there whether anyone saw it or not.

When we finally emerged into daylight—or really into slightly less shady, less thick trees, we had no idea where we were, but there was a big map on top of a stone kiosk. We studied the map and then looked up and scanned the smattering of buildings positioned here and there on the acres of green grass and sculpted flower beds. The stone was a warm golden beige color, and had a slightly sparkly quality when the dappled sunlight flickered on it. It was hard to comprehend that people our own age lived here, although at the moment, there weren't many people around. A couple white kids with backpacks scuttled into a building in the distance. My heart raced, just the way outsiders' hearts probably raced when they came to our neighborhood by mistake.

"It said on their website that half the junior class goes overseas, to, like, Africa and stuff," Valdur said. "Where would you go?"

I could feel my brow furrow, and I turned to look at him. *Where would I go? By myself?* "Man, you're starting to sound like Allison. We've got to get there. Come on."

We ran behind the buildings closest to us, along the tree line, until we got to the Kurtz Administration Building. We skidded to a stop, Valdur bumping into me, and stared at it for a second. "We're here," he said. Then we slapped each other on the back. We brought ourselves closer for a half hand shake, half hug.

But when we got to the top of the steps, and I

tried to pull the door open, it was locked. "Oh shit," said Valdur matter-of-factly. He didn't throw his hands in the air, and he didn't pace and then put his hands on hips and look at the sky and curse God. It's funny, but at that moment, I felt a pang of something dark and ugly. Did college matter more to him than I did? What plans did he have brewing underneath that crazy-ass hair?

"It's lockdown," I said with a shrug, fighting to keep calm. "We just have to wait here for a few minutes until it's over."

Valdur sat down on the step, and I wanted to kick him for his quick compliance.

"Hey look," I said. "That window is open." I went into the grass and stood under it. "We can just go in that way," I said.

"Maybe we should wait," he said.

"There aren't any bars," I pointed out. In our neighborhood, a window without bars was often used like door, people hopping down to street level rather than negotiating the junkies or card games in the apartment hallways.

"I know, but . . . " he said. Then he sighed. He moved under the window, bent his knees a little, and clasped his hands together, indicating that I should put my foot there and he would hoist me up. "You climb in. Then come get me."

"No. Why don't you climb in?"

"You *know* why." He stood up and looked down at me. "I won't fit."

"I am not your bitch, Valdur."

He sighed. "Who said you were anybody's bitch?"

"All right," I said. "Fuck." But my hands shook —whether adrenaline or anger, I couldn't tell.

He got into position again, and I scrambled up, getting my head and arms through the window and struggling to get leverage. I felt Valdur's hand on my ass pushing, and my foot finally found his shoulder and I dropped through the window, landing on the pink tile floor of the ladies room. And now there was a rip in the side seam of my new button down shirt.

"You in?"

"Um, duh," I called back.

I peeked out into the hallway. No one around. I started to run. Where was I going? It was five minutes past the scheduled start of our interview, and I hadn't let Valdur into the building. *Let him wait.* I told myself that I had to find Provost Stevens first and foremost, that nothing else mattered. The place was like a fucking maze. The office numbers weren't in order. Every hallway looked like every other hallway, and I couldn't tell if I'd been in it before. I tried to read the names on the office doors, but my sick pounding heart blurred my vision. I made out Holstein, Jans, Ludwell, Johnson. *Office of the Registrar.* What was a *registrar*? Where the hell was Stevens?

"Stevens!" I yelled. "Dr. Stevens!" My voice reverberated off the cavernous hallway walls. I sounded like a man, my voice low and deep. Though not quite as low and deep as Valdur's. I pictured him outside pacing, I hoped, by the locked door. Maybe now he would see what it would be like to be alone, to be without me. But I was the one who was terrified. "Stevens!" I yelled. "Dr. Carl Stevens!"

I yelled for a while, probably really just a few minutes, though it felt longer—running and running. I didn't know where I was anymore. The place was huge. Finally I stopped to catch my breath. I doubled forward and put my hands on my knees. When I stood up, there was a slight white man at the end of the hallway. He had a crew cut like an astronaut, and he wore a suit. He looked like he might puke. "Just calm down, son," he said. "Whatever the problem is—" He stopped mid sentence like he'd used up all his breath.

"Dr. Stevens?" I said. "Provost Stevens?"

He paused before he answered. "Yes." He closed his eyes for a moment. "Yes. I'm Dr. Stevens." I'd found the open man. We hadn't lost the game.

"Malev Karu," I said, pointing to myself. "I'm sorry I'm late for my interview."

"Jesus," said Dr. Stevens, exhaling with relief and bending over a little at the waist, his hands on his hips. Then he stood upright again and sighed. "Don't you know we're on lockdown here, son?" He came forward and grabbed my arm, his hands shaking. He looked up at me, his shimmering eyes large and kind behind a pair of wire-rimmed glasses. "I thought you were going to shoot me."

"With what?" I said, showing him my palms. "My wallet?"

"Wise guy," he said.

He kept a grip on my arm, guiding me down the hallway as firmly as if *he* were the one who was double *my* size, instead of the other way around. Every now and then, a door cracked open, and I could see a person down near the floor peeking out, just a big scared eye or just a mouth. "What's happening?" voices whispered to Dr. Stevens.

"I don't know yet," he told them. "Just stay put." It was hitting me that they took lockdown much more seriously here than we did at our school. It was a big deal, I saw now, that he had come out to meet me.

Finally we arrived at the double doors to Dr. Stevens' rather grand office, and one of them cracked open before we reached it. An old woman looked up at us from the floor, her face ashen. "Get in here," she hissed. "And shut up."

"My secretary, Lois," he said. "See how she talks to me?" He wandered into the room and collapsed in his maroon leather desk chair. There were numerous degree certificates framed on the wall, and I'd never seen carpet this plush anyplace—not at school, not at home, not in any of the stores near our apartment. No wonder everyone was hanging out on the floor.

Lois shut the door behind me. "Get away from the windows," she said to Dr. Stevens. "You're supposed to be under the desk."

"God, I don't have anymore energy for this," he said, smiling. "I want to die in my comfy chair." He winked at me and picked up the phone. "I'm calling security to let them know you're in here. Where's your brother?"

"I—" It should have been an easy thing to say —that Valdur was outside the locked rear entrance, hopefully cursing under his breath, hopefully trying his vertical leap to get himself through that window instead of sitting on the step, letting the chips of our lives fall where they may.

Was there some part of me that didn't want Valdur to see me in here—a little bitch hiding under a desk? Or was it that I didn't want him to meet a man like Dr. Stevens, a man whose eyes were too shrewd not to know a mismatched set when he saw one?

Either way, the words I said seemed innocent enough. And sometimes, maybe I can even convince myself that they were, that I didn't risk Valdur's life to save my own. With the breath I expended to say, "I don't know," I created *oie,* a wind, a counter-wind, and blew life into a series of events that, deep down, I knew would come to pass—my brother would be picked up outside the building by the campus police, would go to jail all day as a "person of interest," his bruised face on the local news, until the school cleared up the misunderstanding. We would both retreat home to our traumatized mother, who would close the store, shut the shades, and say the rosary until her vocal chords were raw as verivorst. She would forever after sit by the window when Valdur left to drop off a letter at the post office or to buy a Slurpee. None of us—not Valdur, Mother, or I—would ever talk again about this year of basketball.

Dr. Stevens covered the mouth piece, and he studied me. "You lost him?"

And just like that, with a nod of my head, the same head Valdur had touched earlier in the cab, I became the man who lost his better half.

LITTLE BIG SHOW

The footpath gallops ahead like a dumb dog, disappears around bends in the forest. This has been Alexander's first real hike, a hard scrabble—scuttling along in a crouch at times as if he might find grips on the flat rocks. His assistant at work would have *loved* some photos.

Now that he's made it—almost made it—this easy wide dirt path where he and his sister Marietta started hours ago, where families had pushed all-terrain strollers, seems embarrassing somehow. A bird chirps sweet, trilling notes. The watery quality of the sunlight suggests cocktail hour. Through gaps in the trees, the gravel lot materializes, but there's no blotch of red. Marietta's car should be visible. Shouldn't it?

"Hold on," he calls ahead to her. He spins around. "Is this where we started?" He knows it is, even with the trail deserted, other trekkers probably at home now firing up their grills for the Fourth of July like normal people.

"You did it, big guy!" she says, brings fluttery hands to her cheeks as if someone has proposed. He resents her surprise. His wife, his *ex*-wife, began to talk to him like that after they had stillborn twins last year. Like he was a little bit of an idiot.

Yet he hopes Marietta's sunny affection is sincere, the desire a hum in his chest. Since Alexander's divorce, his sister has stopped visiting him up in Baltimore.

Surely in another minute, that stupid Dodge Omni will flicker into existence between the trunks. Pulling ahead of Marietta, he breaks into a trot.

"You're *running!*" she calls after him, and picks up her pace to a jog.

When he bursts from the forest, he stops short at the edge of the gravel clearing as if it's a cliff. Empty. A gray sea of rocks. A spray of broken glass.

Marietta emerges beside him. Her smile drains away.

"Gone," he says. He points to where the car had been, to the parking space she managed to grab hours earlier, when the lot had been full. The trees block the waning afternoon light like a leafy gang of thugs. "My briefcase," he whimpers.

The proposal for the Jamieson account, a proposal he insisted on creating himself instead of letting his staff handle it, was on his laptop. Worked on it for three straight days and didn't get around to backing it up. He's been doing bone-headed things like that ever since this new woman, Nichole, materialized —she shares his table sometimes at Common Ground, an over-crowded coffee shop. It seems impossible that such a thing can happen after he drove his wife away with his drinking and insults, drove her right into the arms of Jimmy Yang, a hotshot systems specialist at a competing agency.

He walks the perimeter, as if he might find the car hiding behind a stump. His chest expands with air. Alexander blinks away the doctor's thick fingers, the way they worked tubes up the twins' noses. He thinks about the dangers of breath. What if his lungs bulge through the gaps between his ribs, press until the bones snap?

Marietta stands at the edge of the clearing, staring blankly up and down the road.

"Maybe someone borrowed it," she says.

It must have been ten miles to Charlottesville. "Even you don't believe that."

She shrugs, shades her eyes, and scans the distance, as if she's deliberating whether she believes it or not.

He studies the pile of glass shards on the gravel where the Omni had been. He slaps his forehead. He throws his arms like he's pitching baseballs. "I'm ruined," he rasps, and he wishes he would stop stomping. But the pain in his feet, although he knows it's there, feels faraway right now, like the possibility that anything will be all right, ever.

Marietta puts a hand on his shoulder. "My yoga teacher says that what we see depends on what we look for."

"Someone jacked your car. I don't think that's subjective."

"You really think so?" She bends over a little at the waist, as if this news is a physical thing, something that has struck her. When she straightens up, day-glo color flushes her cheeks. "My prayers are answered!" she says, a hand on her chest like she's won something. "I've been wed to the wrong car for years."

She's right about that one—the Dodge Omni was a crappy car even during the Reagan administration, when their father bought it new. But old cars are easy to hotwire, and trail heads are quiet places. Good thieves probably aren't connoisseurs.

She pulls the neon wallet from her shorts pocket, and she takes out her driver's license. She studies her own picture like she's seeing herself for the first time. "I've always thought I was meant to be in a classic VW bug," she says. "And see, the universe is making it easy for me."

He nods. But then he can't help himself. "Well,

actually, the insurance policy that Mom and Dad bought you—*that*'s what will make it easy." Their parents have subsidized her for years: a life that consists of expensive massage seminars and a part-time job at the Mystic Sunflower Healing Hands Co-op. What bothers him the most about the way they dote on her is that he suspects she really does deserve it—she's so damn likeable that his friends smile at the mention of her name. Like she's Michael J. Fox or Chewbacca. Except in the body of a statuesque woman.

She doesn't take the bait, the way he wants her to, the way Sherry would have. He misses the security of that, of being locked in a struggle with someone. Instead, Marietta says, in a dreamy voice, "Mom and Dad are *so* awesome."

Alexander grabs his own hair with both hands. It's coarse and overly suggestive, will stand up in two horns now for the rest of the day. There was a time when Sherry would have smoothed it with her palms, kissed his cheek. "What am I going to do?"

"Gotta start walking, big guy." Marietta heads down the road.

"Stop calling me that," he says, not loud enough for her to hear. He's too stunned by the truth of what she's saying—they have to embark on foot.

It is, in fact, also true that she towers over him, even in spite of his horns of hair and the lifts in his loafers. As far as he's aware, Sherry is the only one who knows about those. He wears shoes until the moment he goes to bed, even though he lives alone now, and he almost believes he really is 5'7" instead of 5'5". With the inserts comes the risk of shin splints or hairline fractures. The doctor who fitted them years ago said, "These are strictly for hot dates, not for everyday use." Although he ignores this advice, he does gravitate to sedentary endeavors like online games or, increasingly lately, sitting on bar stools. He doesn't play kickball with his employees in the city league they joined. He no longer considers getting rid of the lifts, like he did when Sherry's belly swelled each day, when he imagined his twin sons would play catch with him behind the suburban house they planned to buy. Behind it, he would also torch off huge illegal fireworks for them, sprinting to a safe distance while the fuse crackled, just like he had for Marietta. Their blond heads and freckled faces are as vivid in his imagination as hers is in his memories— slack-jawed, tilted skyward in the red glow.

That summer he was fifteen, he'd saved his allowance to buy shells from the back of an unmarked truck, an unforgettable display for his seven-year-old sister—the *Burning Rings of Fire*, the *Ladybird,* the *Utter Chaos*, all of it confiscated by a passing patrol car. Marietta cried until he caught her eye and flashed the *Hostile Planet* he'd stowed down the back of his pants. He misses that conspiratorial glance, the way they used to know each other's thoughts.

Ever since the break up with Sherry, Marietta has stopped showing up, vegetables from her garden cradled in her arms. Maybe she'd liked Sherry better than him. After all, Sherry gave those funny sidelong glances, and she welcomed people with music she picked out especially for them. Even on the day they separated, she played *Tangled Up in Blue*, one of Alexander's favorites.

When he suggested this hike today, he'd done it as a way to win Marietta back. "We'll stop at the farmer's market on the way," he'd said, as further enticement. He and Sherry secretly referred to that place as "the rummage sale of inedible food." It had been fun to laugh with her about it, and he could just imagine what she'd say if she heard him *offer* to go there. But if that's what it took, he'd do it.

"Hiking?" Marietta had said. "That is so awesome! And hey, I'll drive so you can work on your projects." She gestured to the briefcase, which he carried on his shoulder by the strap.

A little later, as she drove him to the mountain, some kind of irritating folk duo on the stereo, he put the finishing touches on the proposal. Marietta sang in that gorgeous, lilting voice of hers. He looked up and blinked at the winding mountain road; his heart beat slowly with a warm sense of accomplishment. He allowed himself to bask in the blinding blue summer sky, the treetops still tinged with yellow-green new growth, the earthy smell of the air rushing through the vents. *Let's do things her way,* he thought.

And that was how he ended up on a four-hour diamond trail hike instead of a short nature walk to the ranger station, which, according to the map, had restrooms.

Now he grips his phone like he might be able to give it CPR. *No signal,* it says on the screen. It's the only possession he has. Even his wallet and car keys were in the briefcase.

Ahead, Marietta hums "Sentimental Journey" and bends down to pick some electric blue wildflowers. She's thirty-three, but she looks younger. She looks like she did as a kid, hair in two braids and fine blond hairs on her tanned arms.

Finally, they reach the paved main road. The wind whips up each time a car passes; it batters the back of his head. His hair flaps against his forehead like a toupee. And his feet. God his feet. The blisters. He squeezes his eyes shut, tries not to imagine a life without the lifts—rising from his table with Nichole, two inches shorter than he was the time before, her brow wrinkled in confusion. Screw it, right? He could pretend he wasn't in pain, couldn't he?

When the next truck approaches, Marietta sticks out her thumb. The truck slows, swerves toward the shoulder. "What are you doing?" he says.

"Communicating!" she says.

"This is dangerous." He turns and squints at the silver grill, the two smoke stacks. The driver, an older, bearded man, smiles. He wears a cardigan like a high school guidance counselor. There's nothing but guard rail along the infinity of the road. On the other side of it, a steep embankment of trees rises. It's as if Alexander has found himself within the trough-like pathway of a pinball machine.

"I'm a tai chi brown belt," she says. "Negative energy can become positive."

"He might be a black belt in serial killing."

"Or he could be wonderful."

The man does *seem* wonderful. There's a Support Our Troops sticker on the front window, as well as a pink breast cancer ribbon. But things that seem wonderful rarely turn out to be. Marietta used to follow Alexander from room to room when she was little, and he'd felt important, as if he were responsible for how adorable she was. And now he knows that, fundamentally, he's an ass.

He hesitates a moment and grabs Marietta. He spins her around, in the direction they've been walking, away from the approaching truck. She sighs as he hustles her forward. The truck grumbles, breathes down their necks.

He looks over his shoulder and waves the driver away. Finally, the brakes squeak and the trucker pulls back into the lane, trolling past at five miles per hour and staring. "Don't look at him," Alexander says. His heart races. If the man rolls down his window and makes chit-chat, he'll never get her out of here. And really, he could be a murderer.

She shields her eyes, watches the truck disappear. "That was a missed opportunity."

A belt tightens around his stomach. "Everyone is just waiting to make friends," he says.

"Maybe not with *you*." She has finally taken the bait, but it doesn't feel the way he hoped. It just seems like she's moving further away. Now he's the one following her everywhere.

If only a signal would materialize, cut through the bank of mountains, the thick wall of trees, maybe he'd persuade his assistant, Clara, to grab the spare car keys from his condo and drive down here. This is the weekend of her engagement party, and her whole family is visiting from Michigan. Alexander would be looking at big, big bonus pay. He'd endure her ribbings about "Mr. Hobo" who lost his carpet bag.

If his parents weren't trekking across the US in their motor home—they phoned yesterday from Yellowstone to tell him about a particularly large woodchuck—maybe they'd drive down here with his keys. It's hard to imagine it. He has prided himself on being the successful son who sends repairmen to their house or who emails consumer reports for the best TV.

Is it possible that one day he might allow himself to rely on someone in the same way he relied on Sherry? Lately his brain flashes him images of Nichole, a pediatrician with dark curly hair and a cute, crooked front tooth. Her easy warmth with Alexander and with the coffee baristas comes across as genuine, not flirty or theatrical, the way Sherry could sometimes be. She laughs in the same unselfconscious, open-mouthed way as Marietta—he can picture the two of them laughing together. Once, after Alexander guessed right at a trivia question, she fumbled in her purse and produced a gold star, which she pressed onto his shirt. "Good work!" she said.

Still, Alexander hasn't returned her phone call from last week. What if she admits to watching reality television programs or hoarding cats or, after what happened with Sherry, takes even a passing interest in the men he knows?

Marietta turns down a side road. "What are you doing now?" He tries to sound pleasant. He stops, hands on hips, to survey the green hills that stretch to the horizon.

"You won't let us thumb a ride," she says. Marietta is as close to scowling as she ever gets. "So I'm going to Buck's house. It's closer than mine." Buck is the first serious boyfriend Alexander has heard about in a while—a fifty-something landscaper who lives in a two-room cabin. He rents one of the rooms to a Mexican immigrant couple who have a baby named Guadalupe. Marietta's fridge, back at her shared house, is covered with photos of Guadalupe. Does he have to meet this guy—this *old* guy? Especially today? They're bound to break up, and he can probably just wait it out. "Are you coming?" she says.

"Does Buck have cell service?"

"Do you use Sprint?"

"No."

"Well, probably not, then." She turns away and starts walking.

He follows her another mile. A Walmart tractor trailer comes precariously close, and they both dart toward the guard rail. He tries to get her to smile when he says, "I thought Walmart would kill us one day, but that wasn't how I pictured it happening."

Eventually, he follows her down a winding gravel drive and walks another half mile. Prickly weeds bow over a barbed wire fence, skim his arms like crawling insects. His feet are on fire, and they feel sort of knotty on the bottoms. By the time the cabin comes into view, they're numb, like he's walking on two short boards. He tries not to notice that the cabin looks like an overgrown woodshed rather than like someone's home—a box made from untreated lumber, faded gray in the elements. His throat burns from the hot wind on the highway, and he'll be grateful to sit down anyplace.

Buck greets Marietta on the porch, holding the toddler, and he doesn't look fifty years old. He has a tall lanky physique, a thick head of blondish red hair, and mutton chop sideburns. He looks more like he could be Marietta's brother than Alexander does, with his brown hair and pale skin. Buck's T-shirt says *Spam—It's what's for dinner*. Alexander has thirty-something friends who look older than Buck.

His business partner, Eddie, for example, is bald and has a paunch.

Buck sets down Guadalupe. The girl squeals and totters toward Marietta, who reaches out a steadying hand. She leans down to kiss the girl on the head.

"This is a surprise," says Buck, hugging Marietta, stuffing his hands into the back pockets of her cut-offs. "Couldn't you just eat her up?" he says to Alexander.

He has no idea how to respond. But he has to admit that the two of them look like the cover of a healthy living magazine—both long-limbed, angular, and the golden brown color of pie.

"Guess what? Someone stole my car!" she says, putting her hand up for a high five.

He watches Buck's comprehension of this information transform his expression, reddish eyebrows raising, mouth dropping. "Hey-ho!" says Buck, completing the high five, and pulling her back in for another hug.

He studies Alexander over her shoulder. "Have we met?"

"This is my brother," says Marietta.

"Your brother? I didn't know you had one." They continue to hold one another as they speak, and it's like Alexander isn't here.

"Oh my God." She drops her head back and sighs. "I told you."

"You did?"

"And I told you he was coming to visit this weekend, too. You were going to come over for dinner tonight, remember?"

"Oh. Inez took the truck. Sorry, babe. I guess I forgot."

"You smoke too much weed," she says. "Anyway, it doesn't matter now. You're stuck with us."

"Can I use your phone?" Alexander says. "My wallet was in the car. It's gone."

"Hi," says Buck, finally letting go of Marietta and moving toward him, hand extended. "I'm Buck."

"I know," he says, reaching out his own hand, wondering if anyone is ever going to react with the appropriate horror about the fact that a robbery has occurred.

"And you are?" Buck's handshake is firm, almost too firm—as if his whole body, not just his eyes, is squinting.

"Alexander!" Marietta says with an exasperated gasp. She throws her hands in the air. "For Pete's sake!"

"Right, right." Buck seems not to notice the frustration that Alexander worked to cultivate all day. "Great hair, Alex."

He winces. "*Alexander*," he mutters.

"Well," says Buck. "Come on in. Guadalupe and I have just been making sheep cheese." He picks up the baby and turns to Alexander. "I raise sheep."

"So I hear."

"It's just for fun. My business went public a few years ago. Being a 'Chief Operations Officer,'" Buck says, using finger quotes, "seems to involve a board of rich people paying me to work less than I used to." He laughs.

"Boy," says Alexander. "That's sure not true in the advertising business."

"I bet it's more lucrative than landscaping," Buck says. "Not that I'm complaining."

The kitchen is simply a row of appliances along one wall of what otherwise appears to be a bedroom. An unmade twin bed is against the opposite wall. There's a card table in the middle of the room. Buck puts the toddler down, and she eyes him with the suspicion one might expect from an older child. Her ears are pierced with silver studs, and she holds the refrigerator door to steady herself, wavering every now and then as if the earth itself shifts under her feet.

"Is the phone in here?" Alexander says, trying

not to notice the white stuff in a bowl on the bed—he presumes and hopes it's the sheep cheese.

"Oh, I don't have a phone, not of any kind," says Buck. "Didn't I say that a minute ago?"

"Because you object to the radiation from the cell towers?"

"No. When I'm away from work, I want to be away," he says with a shrug, like it's obvious.

"That was going to be my second guess." Alexander sighs and perches on the unmade bed, trying not to disturb the cheese. Guadalupe narrows her eyes like he might be a shoplifter.

Marietta's entire life, it occurs to him, is like an overbooked KOA campground. "I *need* a phone," he says, using his own eyes to plead with her. Her expression softens.

"Look, let's eat. And then we'll walk up that big hill." She points out the kitchen window at what really looks like another mountain. Beyond the sheep pen, it rises straight up, and the top isn't visible, even when he goes right up to the glass and cranes his neck. "There's cell service at the top," she says. "I can show you the path."

He sighs again. "That sounds convenient." He isn't hungry—the adrenaline from the theft still making him queasy. He closes his eyes and tries not to think about the strangers rifling through his things, their hands on his driver's license. Would they pass it around? Would they all laugh at the short dude with the crazy hair? He also tries to stave off thoughts about the lucrative contract at stake on Monday with Jamieson. He'd have to bring everyone in tomorrow —on a *Sunday*—because of his own stupidity. But what was the alternative? Let Revolution Concepts get the account?

"Will this make you feel better? We can have it with dinner." Buck holds up a chilled bottle of Prosecco, a light layer of condensation on the green glass.

For a moment, there's a real possibility that he might fall into Buck's arms and weep. But then it scares him how much he wants it. He read someplace that a person shouldn't be more eager to drink alcohol than he is to eat a sandwich or have sex with his wife. "Maybe I'll pass."

Buck laughs. "Great. Another health nut." He leans closer, lowers his voice. "I suppose you don't go to McDonald's?"

"I mean, not that often. But I'm not against it."

"If I go there again, she says she'll dump me." Buck puts a hand on Alexander's shoulder. He whispers. "I went *today*, man. I had to feed Guadalupe."

Marietta concocts a lasagna with sheep cheese and with vegetables from the garden. While dinner cooks, Buck takes Alexander outside to meet "the girls"—six full-grown sheep and two lambs. Guadalupe clutches Buck's pant leg, tottering along at a pretty good speed. The sheep continue to graze, only the lambs coming to the fence. "Here," says Buck, handing him a couple apple slices. The lambs nuzzle each other out of the way to get to his hand, and he's afraid he might be bitten in the frenzy. Still, he feels himself smile, and somehow he manages not to withdraw his fingers. Guadalupe laughs and claps, falling into a sitting position when she lets go of Buck's pant leg.

Without thinking, Alexander scoops under her arms and lifts her to her feet. "There you go," he says. She reaches up with a grip stronger than most men's, at least relative to her size, and she grabs his finger for balance, just the way Marietta used to.

"That's Lucy and that's Curly," says Buck with a sigh. "I'm going to cry when I kill these two."

"Why are you going to kill them?" Alexander says, wiping his free hand on his pants. From within Guadalupe's fist, he can feel the waves of her shaky balance.

Buck turns and looks at him. He blinks. "They're lambs."

"That's it?" says Alexander. "That's all there is to it?"

"Well, yeah," says Buck. "Am I missing something?"

When they sit down to eat, Alexander is glad there's no meat in the lasagna. Each time Marietta and Buck sip the Prosecco, he aches for the way he imagines it would make his feet tingle with warmth. Still, even though he hasn't been feeling hungry, he can't shovel it in fast enough. Marietta has always been a great cook. It's just the three of them—Buck has put Guadalupe to bed. Alexander asks for seconds of the bread, ripping a hunk straight from the warm loaf. It's thick and smells like a bakery he frequented in Toulouse when he did his semester abroad in college. Maybe he does like food the same way as he likes booze. His shoulders relax. He worries too much. That's all. He makes problems where there are none.

"I got a postcard from Sherry," Marietta says finally.

"Oh?" he says. He looks up from the bread and forces a smile.

"Four months pregnant!" she says. "Isn't it—"

"Awesome?" he says, as if Sherry's pregnancy with Jimmy Yang's baby is old news. He isn't sure why, but what bothers him the most at this moment is the fact that Sherry is still communicating with his sister. Would it be so terrible for Marietta to drop to her knee, forsake Sherry, pledge loyalty to him. He forces out, "Sherry's staff must have *loved* the timing."

"When you find someone special, you have to put that first," says Marietta with a shrug, turning to Buck and smiling.

A lump blossoms in his throat. He tosses the remaining bread onto his plate. "Sherry is selfish."

"Well, love *is* selfish," says Marietta.

"Except when it can't afford to be," says Buck, picking his teeth.

"*Thank you*," Alexander says, but neither of them seems to hear. They stare at one another across the table. Alexander finally understands why. Marietta has placed an empty Chicken McNugget box on Buck's plate. The two of them begin to argue. Alexander grabs the Prosecco by the neck. They don't seem to notice. Then he throws his napkin down so that he can take it into the bathroom and drink it. It's tiny like a closet, and the slanted ceiling slopes so low that even he finds himself crouching.

When he emerges, Guadalupe is fast asleep on the twin bed, lying on her back, all four limbs sprawled wide and her mouth open. He's a little surprised about the disappointment he feels that he won't spend more time with her.

In the hospital, Sherry insisted they hold their twins. They were perfect—too perfect to be alive and also too perfect to be dead, like rubber dummies of exceptional detail, with tiny nostrils and fingernails. She wanted to name them. But he told her that babies were babies, that they didn't exactly have personalities. The fact that there were two of them made it easier for him to pretend it was true. He'd like to go back and shake himself for being exactly the wrong kind of man.

Across the room, Marietta now sits on Buck's lap at the table. He nuzzles her neck, but they're still arguing, at a whisper. "You can really do better," she hisses. He can't make out the rest or Buck's reply.

"Okay," Alexander says, with a clap. "Ready to go up that mountain?"

"Me and Buck are going to stay here," she says. "We never have the place to ourselves like this. We even have a bed." She squeezes Buck's cheek, a little bit hard.

"But you said the trail was complicated."

"You'll be fine. Just go past the sheep and head

toward the woods. Turn right at the compost pile and kind of curve past it. You'll see a large oak, but don't turn there even though it sort of looks like a path. Walk about thirty feet further and you'll see the little trail there. Don't touch anything because there's poison ivy. Okay?" She stands up and opens the back door. There's a purple twilight descending.

"Don't hurry back," she says, grinning. "Capisce?"

Buck, behind her in his chair, snorts to himself. "Capisce," he says. "Who talks like that?"

Alexander steps across the threshold. "Okay, so it's that way?" He points. He descends from the concrete stoop and pauses and then walks a few more steps.

When he looks back, he sees Buck's slow comprehension that Alexander is leaving, the brow furrowing, the head turning toward Marietta. "I thought Alex might smoke with us," he says.

"We're *not* smoking weed right now," she says. The door slams shut.

Once that rectangle of light is gone, it's darker than he imagined, the mountain obscuring the sunset. He looks at the cell phone. *No signal.* "Okay," he says out loud, and he walks away from the house, past the sheep, which now seem like death row inmates. He can hear every tiny movement—the flick of a nubby tail, the slight shift of a hoof, the chewing of grass. It is hard to picture these animals' violent ends, especially in the shadow of this quiet mountain.

He wanders along the tree line, past the compost heap. The cell phone serves as a flashlight. Finally, inexplicably, he finds the oak and stumbles upon the trail, exactly where Marietta said it would be. He enters the dark canopy of trees as he climbs, the phone guiding the way with its blue light. It's quiet except for his own labored breath and except for the owl that hoots and makes him jump. The throbbing in his feet is like company, like noise.

"Aah!" he yells, when a sticker bush snags his

shirt. He reaches down to remove it and a thorn goes right into his thumb. "Jesus!"

He stumbles forward. The phone battery chirps, so he lets it go dark. At first, everything is black. But then his eyes adjust to the lighter color of the trail, just visible against the dark backdrop of the forest.

He begins to catch glimpses of the lights in the valley below. In the distance, rogue fireworks pop from driveways—always a single whistling orange trail into the sky followed by a small, bright explosion. He remembers something. "Oh no," he says. In his briefcase had been yet another item now lost forever —an aerial shell, contraband from an out-of-state business trip. *Little Big Show*. The packaging was black with neon stars and invading space ships. It had been zipped into an interior pocket all this time, just waiting for his twins' first Fourth of July. It's hard to say whether it's worse if it languishes forever in a discarded briefcase or if the thieves steal the pleasure of watching it ignite into double rings and green sparkling vapor, steal the intimacy of standing next to the people they love, open-mouthed, in the presence of magic.

When he finally climbs onto some boulders at the top, he turns around and sits there for a moment, catches his breath, gazes at the lights of Charlottesville laid out before him, sparkling like diamonds. There are more bootleg fireworks, closer, and he jumps, heart throbbing in time with his feet. The pop also spooks a family of deer. He can just make out their big bodies and graceful legs. Their hooves make little noise as they pick their way across the forest floor.

He pushes the button on the cell phone, and the *No Signal* message is gone. He clicks on his contacts list and the phone chirps again.

He could phone Sherry. Her voice would have that lilt of surprise, like he was her old college roommate, someone no longer relevant. Actually, he isn't even an old friend. Or a new one.

Who he ought to call is Clara, so she can scramble the office for tomorrow. He highlights her number, poised with his thumb. But then he scrolls down at the last minute to Marietta. Maybe he'll dial her just so he can listen to her recording, just so he can imagine her adult voice saying the things he wishes it would, things that would make him feel she adores him the way she did when she was small like Guadalupe and seemed to enjoy nothing so much as gazing up at his face. Maybe she's right that love is selfish. It hasn't occurred to him until tonight that she might be caught up in her own relationship, that her distance might not have much to do with him at all.

What actually happens is that his finger dials Nichole.

While it rings, he sits and wrestles his shoes off, drops them on the ground. He stands on top of the rock in his sock feet, the porous surface massaging his soles.

"Hello?"

He sputters. Then he talks fast like an auctioneer, explaining everything that has happened. "Oh no! That's awful!" she says. "Are you okay?" He can't believe how much he needs this, to hear her concern. The balloon in his chest deflates a little. The phone chirps.

"Alexander?" she says.

A question lingers in his throat. The official Charlottesville fireworks display cracks into the sky now, geysers of light—though from here they are only a few inches above the skyline.

The line goes dead, and he realizes what it is, the thing he keeps wanting to know from everyone he loves: "Are you there?" he says.

GET A GRIP

You hit 40. You quite literally hit it, when your knee gives out and you lunge across the kitchen—flinging a handful of Ikea cutlery and then placing your hand squarely into the green frosting numbers on your birthday cake.

Marilyn, your best friend, appears in the doorway. "What was that?" She's the one who bought the cake, one of those perfectly rectangular jobbies from the supermarket—Marilyn never bakes, or cooks at all, actually, as it would ruin her nails. This particular cake had had an image of a semi-nude man on a bear skin rug. The lettering had said: "Have a Mantastic Birthday, Lisa!" You are like a female version of a confirmed bachelor, the neighborhood's Hugh Hefner-ette, and everyone views you this way. Even your dad, who placed a novelty inflatable boyfriend outside the front door of your garage apartment this morning. When you walked out, you hit it with the storm door and sent it flying across the yard, toward the big house out front, where you could see your dad in his bedroom window waving and smiling. A novelty boyfriend from your dad is exactly the kind of karmic price you pay sometimes for living rent free. The hot June wind pinned the thing to a tree trunk, where he developed a slow leak—the six-pack abs and Hawaiian shorts atrophying before your eyes. It was then that you noticed the handwritten sign taped to his chest: *Lisa, You might be 40, but you're always #1!!*

Now, Marilyn looks at you there on your knees, your hand wrist-deep in cake and she says, in a lilting voice better suited for talking to a four year old, "Lisa, you're going to ruin that fabulous dress. What are you doing?" She's the inquisitive type, that Marilyn, ever the psychologist.

"Oh, not much," you reply. "Just wanted to make sure it was all right." Marilyn usually folds her arms across her chest and frowns when you are sarcastic; she says you use sarcasm the way skunks use their stench, as a defense mechanism, as a way to stay alone. "You're spraying," she likes to say. But this time, she actually laughs.

"And is it?" she says. "Cooked?"

"Hmmm," you say, massaging the cake with your hand, trying to conceal any sign of the throbbing pain in your knee. "Yeah, feels good. Just about right."

"Listen, don't worry," she says, bending down to pick tufts of your cat's hair off her cuffs. "I'll just run down and get another one."

Before you can protest, or even get up, she's grabbed her keys and run out the door in one smooth, lithe motion, everything silvery and sparkling—watch, rings, eye shadow, body glitter. You wonder why you can't accessorize like that or solve problems like that and if it is some kind of genetic defect. Maybe this is why Marilyn has a new boyfriend now while you're still hanging out with your ex, as if the two of you are in a rock band together and have no choice or something.

Are you still in love with each other like Marilyn always says? Well, that would be ridiculous. Thirty-one year-old Jake is your friend, sure, but he is too young to get your jokes about Tony Orlando & Dawn or tube socks. And besides, he already has a new girlfriend named Keira, who's twenty-two and works as a mascot for the local single-A baseball team. Keira is a nice girl. She often brings you banana bread when she comes looking for Jake. Truthfully, the bread is a little dry and eating it makes you think about poor Keira's situation, how sad it is that a young girl like that has to go through life being so plain, with small black eyes and a long face like a donkey or like whatever that animal is that she impersonates at work—a dog or whatever. You don't want to be uncharitable, but you aren't sure what Jake has gotten so excited about. But he says he's happy, and that's all that matters. Right?

You've washed and dried your hands and now you are standing by the sink, looking out the kitchen window at the beautiful birdbath your mother bought years ago, which does not have any whimsical characters decorating its base, and does not have a stone cardinal or cherub protruding from its center —it's just plain granite with sharp, sensuous lines, unapologetic for its functional strength, its elegant simplicity, so like her that you always struggle to take your eyes off it. You close them for a moment and count to three. Then, you turn back to the deflated, concave cake on the counter, picking at the remains, which look like some ruined city. The dark sink hole in the white sugary surface looks angry and deep and is a little like the feeling you have in your chest—you are 40. In 40 years you have never been in a relationship for a whole year, nor have you ever felt anything like tenderness when you have been confronted by blond-haired babies on TV rolling around in reams of toilet paper. You have never had a calling to something greater than yourself—never had a deep urge to provide sanitized water to barefoot people over in West Virginia or to entertain folks with thought-provoking illusions involving playing cards and walnut shells or, like your dad, to divine people's futures from their sweaty, cheese-smelling hands. And this is how you have ended up staying in Catonsville, just outside

Baltimore, and managing your father's statuary business, Big Pat's Granite Ranch, and living in the garage apartment behind your father's house, which in turn, sits behind the half-acre gravel display yard, that legion of white stone creatures—gnomes, deer, squirrels, fairies, dolphins, Jesuses, hedgehogs, gladiators, Alice in Wonderlands, lambs, camels, urinating cherubs, Elvises, frogs, Indian chiefs, gods on the half shell, and a little replica of Jimmy Carter.

Both working and living at the Big Pat's compound, combination house/statuary/palmistry center—tallying the best-sellers (always gnomes), selling leprechauns to undiscerning customers when you've sold out of gnomes, flirting with kind, paunchy married men because they always have single brother-in-laws that sleep on their sofas a little too often—it is all just stuff to do until the real you arrives, the real you that lives deep inside and will emerge one day when a hurricane visits or when your cat gets run over or (and the college-educated part of you hates to admit it) when the right man comes along. You wish you felt called to someplace very far away, like Tibet, where you would experience the bliss of absorption, too busy pursuing enlightenment or panting behind a Sherpa to concern yourself with recording *American Idol* when it conflicts with your dad's other favorite, *It's Me or the Dog*. Oh, the throbbing in your knee is nothing; your chest feels like that sink hole in the cake.

By the time Jake arrives, letting himself in without knocking, you have eaten at least half of the thick gritty icing with a serving spoon, gasping it down almost as if you had no choice, as if you were clearing away rubble, looking for survivors.

"Hey hon, what's the trouble?" Jake says, and you hardly hear him. You are still staring at the cake. He stands beside you, takes your face in his hands, and makes you look at him, but you have trouble processing anything except the fact that the skin under his eyes has no fine papery lines, that there are no pits etched beneath his eye sockets like thumbprints, because he is still, of course, too young for all of that. What the *hell* is he hanging around with you for?

Part of you knows you are as good-looking as guys always tell you, even in spite of the lines and pits. You have something of what made your mother the beauty that she was. But this is not reassuring. This is horrible. Because it is still not enough, and it is fleeting, and you will wake up one morning the dumpy round person that you were as a kid and a lonely teenager, before you discovered aerobics, bouncing and jumping your way into a bathing beauty's body and bad knees at age twenty-seven.

"Lisa," Jake says and snaps his fingers. When you finally see him, really see him, you gasp and grab the front of his shirt and kiss him deeply—in a way you never did even when the two of you were together those six months. Jake works as a youth minister at Shepherd of the Hills Lutheran Church. And all those kids tell him their problems. And he fills the rafters each Sunday with haunting acoustic-guitar renditions of "Holy, Holy, Holy" or "I Come to the Garden Alone." And all of the moms touch his arm when they seek advice on matters they have probably fabricated, their fingers so light, like whispers. Why did you ever let him go?

You collect ex-boyfriends the way some women collect shoes. At first, when you start dating someone, you are breathless with the possibility of the woman you might become. You imagine how you will shape yourself around his contours—which are nobler, wiser, more transcendent than your own. Over the first wine spritzer with a guy, at the O'Charlie's Happy Hour or the Holiday Inn Lounge, you know how it will be—the size and shape of the house you will share with him, the kinds of nights out you will have with his friends, the sort of old couple you will become.

You have, from an imaginary perspective, been the wives of many people, including an architect who took you to live in a converted French farmhouse; a sports reporter who brought you to every game he covered for thirty years, smiling at you and waving during the half-time show, as if those half-clad girls weren't even there; and a fireman for whom you cooked casseroles and learned to like canned corn and mourned after his early and heroic death.

The reality never quite matches up, though. You are more than disappointed, almost annoyed, when you discover on the second date that the architect hates Europe, that the sports reporter quite enjoys those half-clad girls, that the fireman is going to criticize your cooking from the start and took the job he has because he rarely has to attend a fire. It never comes back, that initial excitement.

But is it back now? you wonder as you are kissing Jake. Are you excited about him or are you excited about the prospect of being excited? You savor the taste of the Miller High Life he has been drinking in front of the Orioles game at Phil's apartment—Phil, another ex, through whom you met Jake, this man whose lips now feel so right, whose chest, which you raise your hand to touch, is narrow but firm, with a heart beating strong enough to feel in your fingers.

Jake suddenly realizes what's happening and he drops the gift bag in his hand and he clutches your hips, your back, and he starts kissing you for all he's worth. When Marilyn comes back, you and Jake are on the kitchen table beside the cake. Jake's jeans are around his knees, and your legs are nearly behind your head; your bad left knee is at a strange angle.

"Oh Jesus," you hear Marilyn mutter, and then she fumbles the new cake and drops it. She leaves it there, retreats to the kitchen doorway. "Call me later?" she says. "Don't worry," she adds. "I'll intercept your dad." Count on Marilyn to think of that.

A few minutes later—the two of you have

recovered from the interruption and are moving together with even greater vigor—you're studying Jake's face, sweat trickling down his considerable nose, and you think how there's nothing special about this. It's like brushing your teeth, driving your car, something people do everyday, something that in and of itself has no significance, no matter how long it's been since you last did it. You wrap your legs around Jake's back and match his rhythm. "Oh," he says, looking at you with awe and admiration.

Breathless, you focus your eyes on his, run your finger down the side of his angular jaw and then smooth his dark eyebrows, one and then the other. Bright afternoon light streams through your gauzy kitchen curtains, dust floating in the air over Jake's shoulder. The wet tips of his longish hair are curling, like some 70's heart throb from a poster. He is beautiful, which is more than an observation; it's a feeling. The feeling is in that same place in your chest where the hole is. It's like an air bubble, swelling against your breast bone, swelling like it might burst. This is good. This must be good. "Talk to me," you say. "Tell me something you've never told me before."

"Okay," he says and stops for a moment, looks right into your eyes. There is a long pause. "I think I'm going to marry Keira," he says.

You know that if Marilyn is right and you are secretly in love with Jake, you should feel devastated. But you don't. And the fact that you are not devastated is what you find most devastating of all. Maybe, you tell yourself, your feelings are like the chocolate coins in your mother's dresser drawer, which she denied existed, even when you held them in your palm in front of her eyes. "Nice girls don't eat sweets. And they don't snoop," she had said, tilting your hand so that the coins slid into the waste basket one by one.

You are tempted to let your father read your

palm, something you have never done in spite of his borderline begging. Your dad is in the back office of the statuary now with a big hulking farmer from the Eastern Shore, the blinds drawn, their voices barely whispers. You can picture them in there—the farmer's huge calloused hand laid open on the desk like a butchered animal and your father studying it through his magnifying glass, making surprised noises, glancing every now and then at the farmer's face as if to gauge something. Your dad doesn't charge money for palmistry, despite the fact that you and everyone else have told him he should. Even your late mother, who was the book keeper for the statuary before you, infinitely practical, used to admit he had a talent. Her little pink lips pursed like a French person, she would shake her head and say, "You could just be lucky with these predictions, but I don't believe in luck. So where does that leave things?" Your mother had a teacher's square below her index finger, something that had never made sense to your dad, as your mother wasn't a teacher and didn't have innately teacher-ish, nurturing tendencies. Then, when you were twelve, she had an aneurysm. And, boy, that taught you and your dad a thing or two. "I should have checked her mouse," he always said, even now, even these days. "Why didn't I check it? Why didn't I?" The mouse—as near as you can tell, some fleshy bit of the hand that appears when a person makes a fist—is a sign of health. Whenever you absently clench and catch your dad staring longingly, you release and clamp your open palms to your pant leg. "I'm putting down my dukes, Pops," you say. "I'm a lover, not a fighter."

When the two men come out of the office, the farmer looks pale. Is he swaying a little? Your dad refuses to whitewash bad news like Venus the psychic, who lives out on Route 40. Your dad pats the farmer's shoulder, but the farmer doesn't seem to notice. He moves toward the sunlight with his mouth open, looking a little like a toddler.

"Dad," you say after the farmer has gone.

Your dad is thumbing through his appointment book behind the counter and doesn't look up. "Hmm?"

You are staring at him very hard, trying to will him to pay attention. "One of these days, you're going to get done with a session and someone's going to have a car accident."

"Not that I'm aware of."

"Oh, forget it," you mutter.

"What's that, sweetie?"

"*Nothing.*" This exchange pretty much sums up your relationship with him. You are like characters living on opposite sides of a split screen, like in TV shows when they want to show you what two people are doing at the same time, but in different locations.

Your stomach is a little icy. What if you did let him read your palm? He couldn't really tell you anything shocking, could he? He will tell you that you'll have a long life and that you will be feisty when you're old. It doesn't take a palm reader to tell you that your cat will be the central figure in your activities for the next several years. Could you take your cat if you moved to Tibet? You try to picture her, that little orange face peeking out the top of an orange Buddhist's robe as she prays for the end of suffering. But let's face it. If the cat features prominently, you're not really going anywhere.

You sit on a stool behind the counter and watch your dad open a statuary wholesale catalogue and flip through it. You open your mouth to talk to him, unsure how you will ask. "They have some cute new cowgirls," you comment.

He turns his head and looks at you, raising his glasses and placing them on top of his bald head. His eyes are so white and clear, and the brown irises stare into your own, right into the deepest part of your head. You're his means of clearing his conscience. He is about to tell you what he saw in that man's future: the death of a child, maybe, or the loss of a limb.

Or maybe just a downturn in the price of poultry, the breakdown of a new refrigerator, the tendency to alienate loved ones. He clears his throat. Your stomach now feels like it is full of snow.

You sit on your hands.

It's your idea for everyone to be there at the ballpark on the night Jake pops the question. It's humid, heavy, even at 7:30 p.m., when the first batter is struck out by Cassidy Chesnut, the pitcher for the Greater Baltimore Badgers. The sky is low and gray and it makes the Badgers' uniforms look the super shade of white that your mother used to yell at the television was impossible to achieve. "Tide can't make that happen. The whole space program couldn't make that happen," she would say to the man holding up the blinding T-shirt. You would laugh and she would glance at you sidelong, just the hint of a wry smile on her beautiful lips. She almost never laughed, but this quality didn't make her seem cold. Instead, she was alluring, magnetic.

And now here you are looking at that very shade of white. Magic, it seems, is possible. Marilyn watches you break open peanuts. She occasionally pushes the growing pile of shells closer to you with her black pointy high-heeled shoe. "I can't believe he's doing the scoreboard thing," she whispers. "It's such a cliché."

"It's not going to be the scoreboard," you inform her. "Keira can't see very well through the eye holes of her costume."

"Well, whatever. It's a *baseball game.*"

You see someone waving at you. It's Luke McIntosh, a strapping gym teacher you went on a few dates with last year. His entire apartment was filled with Winnie the Pooh paraphernalia—stuffed animals, figurines, dishes, waste baskets, curtains. You feel as though you should have found it endearing. You didn't. You still feel guilty, and you wave as if he's just come back from the war. "Hey Luke!" you call, and he blows you a kiss.

Marilyn sighs. "The only reason your old boyfriends still like you is that you never give them a chance to get attached."

Jake, who is sitting in front of you with your dad, turns around and looks at Marilyn. "That's not true," he says. "What about me?"

"Don't get me started," she says and rolls her eyes.

You punch Jake's shoulder. "You don't like me," you say. "You're just using me because I'm so handy around the house."

"Move over," says Marilyn. "Here comes Stewart." She raises her hand, fingertips wiggling. Stewart, Marilyn's lawyer boyfriend, marches up the bleachers with a cardboard tray of draft beers. You scoot down one row and park yourself on the other side of your father. Stewart distributes the beers and you take a long swill. Your nose tingles.

Keira is doing a handstand on top of the dugout. She walks the length of the roof on her hands, and then she pops up and takes a bow.

You fish from your purse the giant ring that Jake plans to put on the badger's big cartoon finger during the seventh inning—a concept that was all your idea. You made it for him last night out of yellow pipe cleaners, and the diamond is an ornate sparkly button you found in your father's junk drawer. How long had it been there?

Just then you can sense your father's probing eyes studying your hands. You gasp and fumble the ring. It falls underneath the bleachers. "What are you doing?" you say. "Stop looking."

He looks hurt, like you've slapped him, and you regret the harsh tone you've used.

"I was looking at the button," he says. The two of you have not had a moment like this since the time he backed your car into a statue of Chief

Geronimo that you had already sold, breaking him off at the feet. "Well, don't worry," he says, his lips a tight white line. "As far as I'm concerned, you don't have any hands."

Underneath the bleachers, you wade through empty popcorn boxes and coke cups. They are literally up to your ankles, and you wonder about the likelihood of rats. It's very still, and gnats buzz around your ears and eyes. You swat at them, scanning the ground for any glimpse of yellow, kicking litter as you trudge along.

"Find it?" You spin around to see Jake there.

"Oh," you say. "I was hoping you didn't notice."

"I see all," he says in a spooky voice, imitating a gypsy in a bad 60's horror film the two of you watched the other night.

You smile, but only a little. "Don't worry. I'll find it," you say, resuming your search.

"What are you doing after the game?" he says.

"Look," you say. "There it is." You bend down and snatch the ring from the litter, brushing it off. "Good thing it's so gigantic."

You turn around and walk over to give it to him, and you realize, from his expectant look, that he is still waiting to hear what you're doing after the game. The raised eyebrows, the wrinkle of his forehead. It matters to him. And that is when you understand that the reason his impending engagement doesn't bother you is that you know he is in love with you, not with Keira. You stand in front of him, and it occurs to you that if you hand him this ring, it will be like a proposal. You could get down on one knee with the cartoon ring and say the words in a Porky Pig voice. This actually appeals to you. You think of your parents' marriage and its surprising end—the way your father found your mother at her desk with one hand on her coffee cup and her forehead on the calculator, the way he leaned on you at the hospital with all of his weight.

You extend your hand toward Jake with the ring,

and then when he reaches out to take it, you fumble and drop it. Maybe on purpose this time.

"Frick on a stick," he says. "You are one clumsy mo fo."

You watch him bend down and pick it up. There is a pain behind your eyes, and you wonder what an aneurysm feels like.

"You bought an open-ended round-trip ticket to where?" Jake says, fumbling with a croquet set. The two of you are cleaning out your dad's carport in preparation for the yard sale Jake is having next weekend to help finance his wedding to Keira. He's taken the day off from his job, which seems counter-intuitive.

"Nepal," you say.

"But you're not . . . " he says, laughing. "You're not a traveller." Jake has taken the kids in his group camping all over the Allegheny Mountains, and he used to try, without success, to get you to come along.

He puts the croquet set in the back of his Nissan pickup truck. Then he comes back and stands behind you, giggling to himself in a way that seems a little too meaningful. His teeth are so white, like paint. You want to go someplace where nobody whitens or has mutual funds—not that you think Jake has mutual funds. He probably doesn't, as this would require him to save money instead of spending the whole entire sum of his free time and salary pretending to be a surfer, when there is no surf this side of the Bay Bridge. Windsurfing on ponds in rural Maryland is not the same as surfing. You keep trying to tell him that. That shark-tooth necklace and the arm-band tattoo—they are so misguided.

"I could be a traveller, though," you say now, with more than a hint of irritation. If he can bleach his hair every summer, you can apply for a passport. You are trying to free a length of vacuum cleaner hose from underneath some boxes of photo albums. "Why couldn't I?"

"Well, because you've got more hair products in your bathroom than they sell in the hair salon. Where are you going to find room for all that in your carry-on luggage? And when you get there, what are you going to do, rent a yak?"

Keira bounces up the drive just then. She's wearing very short cut-offs and sparkly green flip flops. In the sun, there are hints of gold in her chestnut hair, which is loosely pulled back in a barrette. You suspect she doesn't use any hair products. Jake doesn't know she's there yet; she is standing near the back of his pickup truck, looking around for him.

"When are you going?" he says to you.

"July 3rd," you grunt, finally pulling the vacuum cleaner hose free and stumbling backwards. The top box falls over onto its side and a few photo albums spill out onto the concrete floor. You hurry to pick them up, but Jake gets there first.

"You'll miss the wedding." He stands, hugs the albums to his chest.

"Huh." You struggle to your feet, mop your brow. "Will I?" He is just the kind of person who might open a photo album that isn't his. You do not want to see your mother's face. You do not want to see that she is the same age that you are now. "What a shame." You smile. You put your hands out, nod for him to give them over. He just stares into your eyes in the same unwavering, ancient way the cat does sometimes, as if he understands things about fear and fire that you never will.

It isn't quiet. A car whooshes past. A leaf blower drones in the distance. His gaze almost emits a sizzle, and your mouth drops open like you might say something.

"Jake?" Keira finally calls.

He turns and smiles, this whole other face. He

deposits the albums with you, and he goes up the driveway, and she slides her arm around him and he dips her and kisses her and it looks so easy. This affection is like high school geometry—there are shapes and angles that you recognize but somehow cannot comprehend or control.

You hurry to put the photo albums back, scooping some dirt and maybe some ants into the box. Then, you run out to the backyard and you drag your mother's birdbath into the carport, where Keira is waiting to give you a bottle of water. "What can I do?" She smiles a little nervously, as she always does around you, something Jake doesn't seem to notice.

"Oh, hi, Keira. You got here just in time. Why don't you take this for me?"

You organize your own going away party. Marilyn gives you a card in which she assures you that your cat will love her more than you by the time you return next month. There is a smiley face that's meant to indicate she's joking, but she is probably right.

Everyone gets pretty drunk on champagne your dad was given by one of his palmistry clients, a guy who won a little money in the lottery on a day your dad said he should play. Your dad takes your wrist, promising not to touch your palm, and closes the clasp of a charm bracelet with little travel icons on it—a camera, the Eiffel Tower, an airplane, a sandal. Marilyn winks, and you understand that she helped him pick it out. Still, his eyes are wet, and you understand what it means, you going away.

While everyone is playing Scrabble in your little living room, triple points for travel words, you sneak into the kitchen and have a long look out the window over the sink. Out there, even though it isn't there anymore, you can see your mother's birdbath in its spot under the oak tree. The birdbath looks different on different days, depending on the weather and the season, the angle of the sun: sometimes the stone is white, sometimes silvery, sometimes gray with sparkly speckles. You feel as though you are the birdbath sometimes, as if the space between you and it has become amorphous, a part of you, just by virtue of the force and frequency of your gaze out this window, year after year. The realization that maybe you will miss the imaginary birdbath more than the people in the other room makes you feel truly sad, for the first time since the day with the cake. You laugh a little, at yourself.

"What are you doing?" Jake says, coming to the refrigerator for a beer, the bottles clanking. You don't turn around. You hear him take the top off and have a swig.

You think maybe what you are doing at this moment is trying your best not to love him. Him or anyone else. Because to select a path would be to reject every other path. Or worse yet, you might select a path only to find it wasn't the one you thought you'd picked, like it went through an industrial complex or became overgrown with poison ivy and sticker bushes and venus flytraps. And then what if it disappeared entirely, like your mother? Not that she was a path. You sigh. It is a bad analogy, but you are beginning to see your own point. Maybe all this time you have thought that it's better to hold your breath and freeze, with your feet motionless in the air above whatever path you're on, lest you make the wrong guess. But this, of course, is impossible, a self-deception.

You turn around to face Jake. "Do you ever think about what happened on my birthday?"

"Man," he says very quietly, shaking his head. He develops a faraway look. "That was pretty crazy, huh?"

"What would happen if I told Keira?"

"She already knows."

"She does? And it's okay?"

"Mostly. I guess." He grins. "There was frosting

all in my hair." The two of you are quiet for a moment. "Man, I wish *I* was going to Nepal," he says.

You are not anxious, like you should be, about the trekking maps you haven't yet bought, or the knee brace, or the Gore-Tex pants. Your suitcase is open on your bed, empty.

You reach over and take a swig of his beer. "That's funny," you say, "because I wish I was marrying you."

You can see the words sink into Jake's brain mid-laugh. They surprise him far more than your birthday kiss did. His face goes slack. His good-for-nothing, too-young-for-you, surfer face. The floor has dropped out of your stomach.

"What about it?" you say. "What if I gave Keira my plane ticket, and you married me instead?"

"Stop fucking with me," Jake whispers, and there is a flash of anger. His nostrils flare.

"God," you say, louder. "That's the best advice I've had in ages." You are aware that your attempts at honesty sound like sarcasm and that you are trapped inside the box of yourself even now that you actually want to get out. You feel the tug of your whole body toward the window, toward the view of the birdbath; you start to turn away.

Jake slides his arm around your waist and stops you. You gasp at the potency of it—there's more feeling in him now, you think, than you've ever felt before. And then in a moment that you will think about for a long time to come, you do something that signals, to him anyway, your final, cutting refusal.

What happens is this: You show him your palm. You raise it right in front of his eyes, fingers toward the sky just the way your father taught you, so that it is upright, so that he can see its pinkness, the fragile braided lines that reveal your life, its tender center. You hold it there, still and strong, so that he can see the heart line that, like Geronimo, breaks in half.

HOMECOMING

On Tuesday during lunchroom duty at St Luke's High School, where he teaches history, Ned gets a hard-on. He slides into the familiar blue pool of his body for the first time since his father died. What happens is this: he's on watch at the door for unlawful food smuggling, scanning the room, when he spots Margot, his ex-wife and the principal of the school, who has just returned to Baltimore after a four-week exchange with a principal in Southern California. She is Margot, but not Margot. She's a freckled stranger with a new nose piercing. A tiny diamond that glints like love.

Margot eats butterscotch pudding at the teachers' table on the other side of the cafeteria, amid the noise and catsup and restlessness. Eating here is part of her campaign to tear down the boundaries between the students and staff at St Luke's High, boundaries Ned has always rather liked. They're comforting, like the metal detectors. Like telling Margot she's wrong.

At forty-one, she is an absolute knockout—not a knockout "for her age" but a pure knockout. There are sixteen year-olds at the school who stutter when she greets them in the halls. Not that Ned really noticed all that after he married Sally last year. Something—maybe that unbelievably hot piercing?—peels a film from his eyeballs, and his vision fills him to his toenails. This boner could cost him his job—how fitting would *that* be?

He studies the dark wavy of her hair, and that light brown skin, dappled with fresh freckles. At the table closest to Ned, two boys hock mucus into each other's milk cartons. He could punish them with detention, but he ignores them, just as he ignores the group of girls from the Thespian Society who squeal and jump up and down at the lunch counter, as well as the girls from the basketball team in line behind them, mocking the other girls by fake-squealing and fake-jumping.

Margot sits there with her back to the long row of windows with bars on them, her posture straight and elegant like she should be in Louisville at Churchill Downs wearing white gloves and a hat with real flowers on it. And anyone could see that when she rises from her chair she will be six feet tall. Something about the sun-drenched color of her hands, he thinks. Or maybe it's just the hands themselves—wide and flat with a graceful grip around the spoon that delivers the pudding. Something about the way she holds her fingers makes him recall the last time they made love, twenty-three months ago, after the divorce was final and just before he met Sally. He allows the memory to roll through him. Those fingers, their tender tips under his shirt, on his chest, his stomach, the gentle firm of them as they slide into his boxer shorts. That touch on his skin kick-starts him, like nearly drowning. Ned gasps. Is he having a moment of divine insight, like the persecuted heroes in his *The Pageant of History and You* textbook?

Theirs was not one of those shocking divorces; no one said, "But they seemed so happy!" Ned and Margot had courted intensely at the end of college, married, had their daughter Ellie, and then proceeded with their marriage as if it were a cut-throat—but amateur—tennis match. They both had affairs, reckless shots at each other that left them off-balance, and on the rare occasions that they attended parties or dinners together, they made jokes at one another's expense, volleying back and forth until people began leaving the room. The most surprising thing about their divorce, even to their own teenage daughter, is that it came so late. In a literal sense, Ned hasn't really *known* Margot for years, which somehow makes his ability to conjure up intimate images of her seem very wrong. But he won't say, at this moment, that he's sorry he can.

Margot tilts her head closer to Madame Sanders, the French teacher. He can almost smell her neck, the tangy sweet of her apple body lotion, and cold trickles along the hairs on his arms. Maybe yesterday's accident has jarred something loose, allowed him to feel something hidden in himself, and he reaches toward the bandages under his slacks on his shin and thigh, the wounds that burn, as if his whole body is waking.

It's that time in the fall when the Maryland leaves have turned the color of the setting sun, the one his father had said reminded him of Ned's mother's hair. She died of cancer when Ned was a toddler, and that particular shade of auburn, pointed out again and again by his father, has been one of the only ways Ned connects with her.

So yesterday, unable to stop thinking about both of his parents being gone, Ned decided to exercise alone, to take his road bike out along a long, twisting route through Druid Hill Park and the wooded Jones Falls instead of going to the weight room with Coach Mike Lester and some of his football players, as he normally does when he finishes teaching; as a veteran teacher, Ned has his prep hour the last period of the day and can leave early when he wants. On many days, when he's had to lecture to mouthy sophomores all afternoon, his spirits get a boost from outlifting all but the strongest linemen on Mike's varsity team.

About seven miles from home, the brakes on his bike locked as he tried to slow down on a sharp curve. In a long, rational moment, he knew that the best action he could take would be to go into a slide, staying close to the pavement by kicking loose from his toe clips and shoving the bike away from his body, but he'd understood that instead he was going to fly over the handlebars, which is exactly what he did, his anchored feet pulling his pedals and then the rest of the bike off the asphalt. His body twisted in the air toward the center stripe. A car appeared in the opposite lane, a pale blue Mercedes with a metal grill, maybe an old one, 1972 or 1973. Ned's mind produced a flitting, precise calculation: Given his trajectory and the significant mass and velocity of the Mercedes, he was about to become flat and probably dead. He landed on his side, his arm under him, his head somehow not striking the ground. In what must have taken less than a second, sprawled there on the asphalt, he watched the car swerve. The complex topography of the tire tread approached his face. It was just a few inches away when it turned.

The driver of the car, probably terrified by what almost happened, didn't stop, and shaking with adrenaline, Ned lifted himself and his bike off the ground. He straightened his seat, turned sideways by the impact, put the limp chain back on the gears, and continued cycling. He looped back on another road to his neighborhood. Only when some children stopped their games in the piles of leaves to stare did he look down. A raw pink spray of road scrapes ran the length of his leg, and a several-inch gash soaked his sock with blood, a rivulet of it still flowing. He felt little, hardly any pain at all. Until now, until Margot.

He pretends to brush off some lint—how visible is the action in his slacks? Thank God it's laundry day. His underwear are old and a little tight, clamping him down. This whole thing is also a welcome surprise, though—he has been having problems in this department for some time. Is Margot looking at him? She grins, gives a dainty wave, fingers wiggling. Her mouth goes pouty. Maybe she is about to blow him a kiss. But just then a teacher leans across the table to ask her something. She leans to one side and continues to smile at Ned over the teacher's shoulder. Exhilarated, he smiles back, too much even—his cheeks hurt. He sees but doesn't see Ivor Griffiths and Samson Peterson, juniors from his third period, who command the table in front of Margot's, grinning back and pointing at their vintage Metallica T-shirts, which they mistakenly believe he appreciates.

Then Ned looks around the teeming cafeteria for Mike Lester. Right now is the rare occasion when he feels like talking to someone, but Mike is the only person, aside from Sally, who knows what's been happening—that he has felt for months like he has been watching his life through a window. Or maybe, he thinks now, it's simply that he has wished it weren't his life, because in this life he has, he doesn't have Margot. It's strange to think that he hasn't realized how crucial she still is. The longing for her is a sensation as acute now as the long, serrated gashes on his leg.

But Mike is nowhere to be seen, is probably already out on the patchy field with his fourth period class shouting, "For the love of Christ, pick up your feet!" Gym is the only class students care as little about as history, a state of affairs that Ned and Mike often discuss over beers at the Sharky's Pub happy hour. During Ned's history classes, the students gripe that the material is irrelevant to their lives; they fidget. Mike loves to egg on the whiners, the ones who complain they have been committed to a Nazi labor camp, as if the injustice of elevating their heart rates is criminal—though in truth they read so little history that Ned often wonders if they would recognize a Nazi in full regalia, goose stepping around the St Luke's High School baseball diamond.

At this moment, however, Ned would tell Mike that he doesn't mind all that. When he and Margot again lock eyes across the room, his lower body crackles like a firework, expands and spirals, and it is enough that he, Ned Harrison, is alive.

That night, after he makes love with a pleasantly surprised Sally, Ned realizes that maybe he's facing an entirely different problem now. In the dark, he stares at the yellow valances on the window, at the open blinds, at the very tops of the shrubs he and Sally planted behind their row house. His legs are still tangled with hers and with the sheets, the film of sweat on his skin just now growing cold. Her breathing has slowed to a regular rhythm. He casts his eyes along the length of the room, lets them rest on the boxes of yearbooks and trophies in the corner, things they still haven't unpacked in the year they've lived in this house. Is it a sign? Maybe, he thinks, Sally has simply been serving as a Margot substitute. If he is honest with himself, he has to admit he has been picturing Margot tonight. The realization keeps him awake after Sally drifts off, her head on his chest and her arm draped over his lean abdomen—he's not so bad himself at forty-two. He touches her hair. Maybe if he touches her head, he can connect with what's inside it.

They have only been married a year. They met at a dance-a-thon that raised money for lower-income youths to go to college, and Ned has always thought that was the right kind of circumstance to meet someone solid—and most of the time, he's thought Sally is the most amazing person he has ever known. She works in a hospice for the terminally ill, and while she might not have the athletic habits he does, or—he admits it to himself now—the stunning body of Margot—emotionally she has the strength of an ox, something that drew him to her immediately. Ned's father didn't die a long, painful death like Sally's patients; he dropped dead of a heart attack on his riding lawn mower. But somehow Sally still knew exactly how to handle everything. She mostly left Ned alone during the few days leading up to the funeral, but she gave him chores to do that occupied him a little, like cleaning the gutters and refinishing a bookcase. Then one night after the funeral, while they were watching the news about a bombing someplace far away, she took his arm and draped it over her shoulder. And even though he hadn't ever cried in front of Margot, he had broken down with Sally. His father, who had been the football coach at St Luke's High School for thirty years, would have told him to stop being such a girl. Mike would have punched him in the shoulder and walked out of the room, embarrassed.

Ned moves his hand to Sally's back, and her bones feel small and bird-like. When she's awake she seems so much bigger than 5'3". He thinks now, lying on his back in the dark, staring out the window at the swollen harvest moon in the city sky, that maybe he married her because she seemed, in every way, to be endless. Unlike his mother, who died when he was three. Unlike his father, who was only endless when it came to expecting excellence on the football field, who was disappointed with Ned for only making the second-team all-state squad. Unlike Margot, who had endless demands of herself when it came to her career—giving everything to her students and staff—and reserved nothing to give to him.

He concentrates on the steady rhythm of Sally's breath and it lulls him to sleep.

By Thursday, the big gash above the knee on Ned's right leg becomes infected. The leg swells like a plump, tight sausage, and he finds himself limping through the halls between classes.

"So, whose ass did you kick?" Mike Lester says when Ned limps into the faculty lounge for lunch, his one-week stint on cafeteria patrol over.

"Mine, I think," Ned says.

"Let me have a look at that," Mike says and gestures to an armchair in the corner, away from the table in the middle of the room, where Mrs. Aziz, an English teacher, and Miss Field, a biology teacher, are sharing a meal of carrot sticks and talking about a new video game chock-full of obscene phrases that all of the kids are quoting during class.

Mike was once a physical trainer for a professional soccer team up in Philadelphia, but he gave it up for the chance to return to Baltimore and coach the football team after Ned's father retired. Mike was three years behind Ned in school, and so they had known each other only by gridiron reputation—Ned the star defensive back, punter, and coach's son, Mike, the freshman squad's quarterback, already acknowledged as savior of the next season's varsity team. Now he pushes up Ned's pant leg, carefully unwraps the ace bandage, and winces when he sees the wounds that run from Ned's shin up to his thigh, and the almost purple gash, still open, next to his knee. "Christ," he whispers, glancing over his shoulder at Mrs. Aziz and Miss Field. He gently touches Ned's oozing skin. "What the hell have you done to yourself?"

"Remember that bike wreck?"

"You did a horrible job cleaning it out," Mike says. "It reeks. You need antibiotics."

Ned feels strangely at one with his numb, misshapen leg, and he isn't as alarmed as he knows he should be. "I know," he says.

"With an infection like this, you can actually lose toes, or worse if you let it go long enough." Mike rewraps the bandage and adjusts Ned's pant leg and then he looks at Ned. "You're all pale. You feel a little woozy?"

"No. I'm fine," Ned says, but he's lying. He has been a little dizzy all day, and probably running a fever, though he hasn't correlated it to his leg necessarily. Maybe this is just the excitement of the new him, the new Ned, he has thought.

"That's good," Mike says and he goes across the room to the sink and washes his hands. "Go to the doctor," he says to Ned, over the heads of the two teachers at the table. "It's more than I can deal with."

"What time is the game tomorrow?" Ned asks, changing the subject, thinking of Margot, knowing she'll be there to greet parents and mingle with alumni. He hasn't told anyone about his renewed feelings for her, not even Mike. But he can't stop thinking about the look he and Margot shared in the cafeteria on Tuesday. This week is Homecoming, and the St Luke's Celtics are playing their oldest rivals, the Baltimore Polytechnic Institute Parrots.

Maybe he'll talk to Margot as the band plays at halftime. She'll look at him the way she did the other day, only better—unfettered, without interruptions. She'll gaze at him like he is a new and wonderful discovery—an uncharted planet or a cure for a disease. He cannot imagine what he is saying to her or what she's saying to him, only the happy music of the marching band, and then he kisses her, and she is so limber in his arms, in a way she never was before, as if maybe they will dance, and they will both know the steps, like people in a movie. He feels a little guilty for not saying anything to Mike. Maybe his thoughts about Margot are transparent. Maybe Mike and everyone else at school already know. He almost wants them to.

"The game's at seven," Mike says, plucking a brown paper towel from the metal dispenser on the wall and drying his hands. "Like they always are." He stuffs the wadded paper towel into a trashcan with a swinging lid. "Why don't you come down and watch from the sidelines?" He smiles, which extends the lines on his tan, handsome face. "It'll keep you from getting swarmed by all the old-timers wanting to talk to you about your dad."

"It's my week to have Ellie. She'll be with me," Ned says.

"Bring her. It'll be good for her to be around a bunch of sweaty jocks. She probably doesn't remember what boys look like." Since kindergarten, Ellie has attended an all-girls Catholic school, the same one Margot went to.

"That was her mother's whole idea," Ned jokes. He finds Ellie's separation from boys both a relief and something to worry about.

"I hear that, brother," Mike says and gives Ned a high five. Mike's twin ten-year-old daughters sometimes—holding hands—sneak into the locker room after the games for a peek. Mike's wife left without warning a few years earlier, and now he has a live-in girlfriend who's great in the sack but not very good with children. He has to bring them to practice some days, even to Saturday-morning films with his assistant coaches. "Maybe Ellie can keep an eye on the girls," Mike says, "keep them out of trouble."

Ned thinks of Ellie's almost scary knack for staying out of trouble. If kids usually rebel against their parents' values, try to be their parents' opposites, he wonders what Ellie's behavior is suggesting about his life, or Margot's life. Of course, now there are parts of Margot's life he knows nothing about. He's glad she has never remarried. "Hey," he says now to Mike, and he lets out a laugh that sounds, to his own ear, high-pitched and weird. "I'll tell you something funny about Margot." Warmth spreads up his neck. He isn't sure what he's going to say.

Mike doesn't look up. Mrs. Aziz and Miss Field have left the lounge, and the two men have taken the empty spaces at the table. Mike is across from Ned, unpacking his sack lunch—two sandwiches, two apples, two bananas. "That nose ring?" Mike says, taking a bite of his apple. "What a hypocrite. Not that she'll notice." He rolls his eyes. "She's such an ice queen."

Ned knows Mike first took up this opinion out of loyalty to him, but now the statement leaves him breathless. His friend's words recall the way Margot looked at him that last morning, when he'd tried to come home at 6 a.m. Her hair mussed, her face stoic and impenetrable, she had stood blocking the front doorway, using every inch of her height. He had thought at the time that it was disgust he saw in her eyes, and he had slinked away from her, from the marriage, without another word, letting her unspoken point carry the day. Even when they'd made love that final time after the divorce, in his car outside the lawyer's office, she seemed distant, unaffected, like it was one more formality in the proceedings, to duck out of the rain into his car and wait for him to lean toward her. But now he wonders if maybe he was wrong that final morning. Now, he knows, in a way he hasn't before, that people hide inside themselves and outside themselves, as if they are avoiding enemy fire, as if they are at war. He thinks how Sally, who seems so strong, sometimes cries later when she can do so privately, after the patient has died and after the family has left and after she has come home and taken a bath. That's when she cries—alone and clean and sitting on the toilet lid.

"So what were you going to say about her? Our principal the ice queen, I mean," Mike says, lobbing his apple core six feet into the trashcan. The swinging lid flies around in a complete circle.

Maybe, Ned thinks, Margot has never been what she seems. Maybe back then she had really been disgusted not with Ned but with herself, for loving him. Maybe what she had really wanted was for him to force his way back into the house, to care that much. Now there's no way to know. "Oh, just the same as what you said. She looks like a new woman. She doesn't look like your typical Baltimore woman, that's for sure." Ned leaves Mike at the table and throws his uneaten lunch in the trashcan; this thought—the regret—makes him feel a little sick. He tries to shake it off as he limps down the hallway, on his way back to class.

When Thursday night comes, Ned still hasn't been to the doctor. Strange dark patches have appeared, and there's more than a tingling now. A burning, a spiral of pulsating pain rises from just below his knee all the way up to his groin. The bad leg is nearly twice the size of the good one. But he hasn't gone to the doctor, and in order to hide his leg from Sally, who could probably fix it up some, he's been changing his clothes in the bathroom. He lies awake just concentrating on the leg, not because he likes the sensations there exactly, but because the pain tells him he's still awake to his life. He's so focused on the leg, and its connection to Margot, that he hardly touches Sally, though he notices the pang of guilt that he feels for ignoring her, like a fluttering moth in his chest. He would admit it if confronted: he has been behaving strangely.

As if she can read his thoughts, Sally rolls over to face him in the dark. "Is anything wrong?" she says. From the faint light at the windows, he can make out her eyes, her petite mouth, the worried wrinkles of her forehead.

"The opposite," Ned says. "The students actually seemed to enjoy my class today—*history* class," he adds. "Some of them even stayed after to talk to me." He knows this is not what Sally was asking.

She looks at him blankly and then she rubs his arm and then his stomach, his chest. "That's not so surprising," she says. "You're a good teacher."

That tired bit of praise sounds a false note. "No I'm not," he snaps, shrugging off her hand. "I don't even know why I became a teacher. Maybe just because I thought it would make the old man a little bit fucking happy." Ned is surprised by what he's said, unsure if any of it is even true. Is he any different from the other teachers, with their cardigans and frizzy hair and uncanny knack for reducing complex subjects to the size of a worksheet? Had his dad even cared, once he had quit football, whether Ned became a teacher instead of a state trooper or a Microsoft executive or a gas station attendant? Has Ned hung around all these years simply because he liked to *imagine* his father wanted him to? And why does it feel as though it's Sally's fault that he's thinking about all of this stuff? "Why are you patronizing me?"

She looks hurt. "Jesus Christ, Ned," she says. "Get a grip." She rolls over and faces the wall again. After a while, she sighs. "And once you do, would you just go to the fucking hospital?"

They don't speak after that. Shadows gnaw on the walls; he tries to let the rhythm of Sally's breath lull him to sleep. It doesn't work.

On the way to the game on Friday, Ned stops by the hospice because Ellie wants to drop off a sandwich for Sally. The hospice is actually the left half of Our Redeemer Baptist Church, which the pastor sold off in order to stay afloat. There are two front doors now, but otherwise the old white building with the steeple is exactly as it was when Ned was a boy. He waits outside in his green Bronco, thinking of Margot, the engine running, his leg hot, the skin beginning to crack now from the days of swelling. He hopes Ellie hasn't noticed that he's been driving with his left foot. He knows she won't ascribe his reluctance to go inside the hospice to his sore leg. Though he's never said so out loud, Ned has always hated the hospice, and hardly ever steps across its threshold. It smells bad. He always feels incompetent there; he doesn't know anything about sick people and can't begin to guess what to say to their families, who camp out in the rooms and halls like refugees. There's a part of him—though he knows this doesn't make any sense—that feels embarrassed for them, like dying is some kind of mistake, a failure. What makes it all worse is that Sally and Ellie always seem to know exactly what to say and how to act. Even Ellie, who never speaks, becomes this warm, gracious Princess Diana kind of person. Has she learned it from Sally in the brief time they've known each other? Why hasn't he learned how to be more like that himself?

Ellie runs back to the car, her wavy dark hair blowing back, her red pea coat flapping awkwardly, and Ned can see in her timid eyes that hint of Princess Diana, just wearing off. "So, how's Mr. Hammond?" Ned says. He never asks about the patients, certainly not by name. He has always believed that speaking their names would bring bad luck. Sort of guilt by association.

Ellie looks at him with surprise and then adjusts her coat underneath her. "He's not doing very well," she says. "Some people in his family have stopped coming because they can't handle it."

"That's sad," says Ned.

"That's people," says Ellie. His daughter's face is like her mother's, with light brown skin and freckles and hazel eyes, but she has Ned's full lips.

"When we get there, do you want to get an ice cream? Or popcorn?" Ned says. He pretends to play with the radio for a moment as he manipulates his left foot over his rigid right leg and onto the accelerator. He finds a song on the radio that he likes, though he doesn't know the band.

Ellie stares at him blankly. "You're singing," she says. "You never sing."

Ned grins. He lunges to her side of the car and kisses her forehead, leaving behind a glistening wet spot. "Everything is fantastic!" he says. Just then, a car sporting St Luke's flags speeds past on the road. Ned rolls down the window, thrusts his fist into the air and yells, "Whoooo!" His voice spirals into the cold air like a siren, and even the meth addicts, clustered on the other side of the road, turn to look. The car honks in acknowledgment. He can see people smiling inside it and he laughs.

But Ellie is leaning toward her door as if the noise has hurt her, or as if he might try to kiss her again. She gives him a puzzled half smile. As Ned organizes his feet on the pedals and begins to pull away, Ellie waves at an old man standing by the hospice's front door. "Oh, I forgot," she says. "Sally told me to tell you that you're an idiot." Ellie says this as if it's a question, as if Ned will be able to explain the message. When he doesn't, she shakes her head and sighs like she is disappointed about the whole affair. After a moment, she looks at Ned and raises her own fist half-heartedly. "Go Celtics," she says. "Are we even going to make it to the game?"

Near half-time, the St Luke's Celtics are down by seven, lucky they aren't down twenty-one, and tempers are running high. There are so many alumni at the game that the bleachers are full and people are standing all along the chain link fence that separates the bleachers from the field; fights have broken out with some of the more boisterous Poly Parrots fans. After one play, when the Parrots block a field-goal attempt, a cornerback's father calls Mike a "wuss" and throws a beer bottle. He resists security, flailing and yelling Mike's name when they hustle him out. Mike asks an assistant coach to stand behind him and watch the crowd so that he won't give the man's sympathizers the satisfaction of booing him to his face.

Ned watched these games from the sidelines from the time he was seven until he was fifteen, and never saw anyone do anything like this to his father. Those were different times. People looked at Ned's father like he was more than human, like even when he was losing, he did so to fulfill a plan for the future of St Luke's football that transcended their understanding. When was it that people stopped having that kind of faith in the things they loved? Ned can picture his father's stocky form, his green ball cap, the clipboard he held during games, though no one knew that the paper on it was always blank. He can still see the stern way his father chewed gum when he was concentrating and the small modest smile he gave Bobby Rhimes, the local TV news reporter, when they stood together in the bright artificial lights after the players had jogged off to the locker room. But most of all he can still feel his own childhood awe of the man, like the feeling you have looking off a giant cliff or at a wild animal that you try to edge closer and closer to, awe that remained even when Ned had grown almost to manhood, when he had become part of the story, and Bobby Rhimes was interviewing him, too.

At the half-time signal, Mike takes the team into the locker room to regroup, and the dense green and white crowd in the stands seems to breathe for the first time in forty-five minutes. People scatter toward the shoe-box-shaped school building to use the restrooms and to linger in its dark doorways and smoke. Boys poke the ribs of girls who lean over the fence to pass sweatshirts and water bottles to their friends on the cheerleading squad.

While the marching band does several numbers from *The Wiz*, Mike's twins dance up and down the sidelines under Ellie's watch. Ned leaves them there and walks toward the end zone so that he can get to the other side of the fence and double back to the cinderblock concessions stand in the gravel lot behind the bleachers. He cuts through the line of rumbling Corvette convertibles that waits to enter the stadium, each car sporting a Homecoming Queen candidate in a glittering strapless dress and a swept-up hairdo. The girls aren't smiling; no one can see them yet. Shauna Washington, one of Ned's best students, has her hand down the front of her dress and is shifting things around. Monique Seymour, Shauna's less-brainy friend, is leaning over the door of her car and spitting into the grass. Ned doesn't say hello to either of them.

He knows that by now Margot will be buying snacks from the booster club running concessions, maybe a snow cone or cotton candy, something festive and celebratory. He tries to walk as if there aren't bright tentacles of pain gripping his leg, shooting up into his torso, and he looks into the stands at the familiar faces of his students and the older, worn faces of their parents, people he went to school with, the people they married. No one's really a stranger, and he wonders if they can tell what he's experiencing, wonders if they're hiding something, too, and wonders what it might be.

As he approaches the concessions stand line, the colorful snake of green and white, he searches furtively for Margot, hurrying past shuffling retirees, stepping around clumps of students. He is no different from the lost, wandering teenagers trying to find each other—hoping for what? For a glance or, best of all, an intentional touch—some tangible way to exorcise the sensations that bulge and rumble like he's a volcano. Ned doesn't remember having any of this juvenile angst when he was actually with Margot. But then he supposes, feelings haven't really been his strong suit.

When Ned finds her near the front of the line, she's wearing a green fleece sweatshirt and a "Go Celtics!" pin. Margot has always looked good in green, as though the school colors had been designed for her administration, and Ned stares at her wavy chin-length hair and those eyes, like Ellie's, a color neither brown, nor gray, nor green. Her breath comes out in a frosty puff in the cold October air.

"Ned!" she says, waving. She's smiling that big

smile at him again. Then, she points to his limp. "What happened?"

"Old age," he says. "Have you seen my cane?" He stuffs his hands in his pockets; he is strangely excited that she has noticed. "Actually, a little bike wreck."

"It's nothing serious, I hope," says Margot.

"Just injured pride," Ned says. "It turned out the road was rougher around the edges than I was."

Margot laughs. It is then that Ned notices the man slightly behind Margot, who for a moment puts his hand to her back—he is handsome, white and dark-haired like Ned, but he's younger, in his mid-thirties, and taller. Ned tries to scrutinize him further, make sense of his expensively casual clothes, but there's a sudden, sharp stab in his abdomen, and he begins to sway and he can't quite lock his eyes on the guy.

Margot notices either Ned's pain or his confusion. "Oh," she says. "Ned, this is Travis." She pulls the man forward and gazes at him for a moment, as if she is amazed herself by his presence. She grins. "I met Travis on that exchange in California."

Travis shakes Ned's hand. The man's palm and fingers are supple, like Margot's used to be after a manicure. Ned squints, wills himself to focus.

"Margot was so inspiring, the way she talked about life in Baltimore, I had to see this place for myself," Travis says, grinning back at Margot. He's got straight, unnaturally white teeth, like he's a celebrity advocate for some kind of good cause—The Society for the Prevention of Corns or something. He has dark eyes and a mole on his cheek, like Marilyn Monroe. "Some game, huh?" says Travis. It appears that Travis has no idea what Ned's tie to Margot is.

While Margot orders her food, Ned stands still, trying to make it clear to both of them that he's waiting to speak to her. He offers Travis a polite smile every now and then to fill the pointed silence. Who the hell is this guy?

After Margot finishes, she tries to give Travis the change from the cashier. He refuses, but takes the nachos, cotton candy, and drinks. "I'll take this stuff back to our seats," he says to her. He nods to Ned. "I love your town, buddy."

Ned smiles, and then looks at the ground. Something about the cotton candy sets him off. Does this guy actually think he knows Margot, that he is qualified to buy snacks with her?

"I'll be right there," she says.

"No hurry," Travis says, flashing that smile again. "You know where to find me." He strolls away like he's on a boardwalk.

"Okay, what's up, Ned?" Margot says.

"Don't you think he's a little young for you?" Strange spots hover like insects in the periphery of Ned's vision.

Margot stares at him for a long moment. "You're jealous?" she says.

Ned says nothing. Now his leg is cold and his stomach feels hot.

Margot is grinning at him in just the same lingering way as she did in the cafeteria, her lips red and her lovely teeth straight and white. She is in love, but the object of her affection is Travis, Ned now realizes, not him. "You know, Ned, this is good. It's payback for—what was her name?—Tiffany? Only, Travis has a lot more money than that little girl." She turns and waves to the parent of an honor roll student, who is walking back to the bleachers with an armful of St Luke's Celtics sweatshirts. "Hey Tom!" she says. He smiles back, waves one of the sweatshirts in the air. Then she brings her attention back to Ned. She has a breezy air about her, arms folded, one hip jutting out, like it's just an old joke, like none of it really matters. But they have never spoken about Tiffany before.

"Mike's right," he hears himself tell her. "You are a complete ice queen." Normally, when they are together, they laugh. They punch each other on the arm, ignoring, basically, their shared history. But this doesn't seem funny. Tiffany had been that final straw in their marriage. She was a twenty-four-year-old temp in the main office, and Ned had slept with her because, he thinks now, he thought it could hurt Margot. In retaliation for what? For making him feel vulnerable maybe?

He had never understood how permanent it would be when Margot was gone. He thinks there is a part of him that has continued to think that he could in some way affect Margot still, that she remains partially his, and he realizes now that this isn't true, any more than his father is still his. Or was ever his. And suddenly he realizes that the two of them, Margot and his father, have always been bound together in his mind, both larger than life, both so far away, even when he has been at his best.

"Is this some kind of fling you're having?" Ned whispers, and he can feel the anger bubbling in his stomach. "A fling with the toy boy? The plastic West Coast asshole? He doesn't belong here."

She slowly comprehends that it isn't a joke. "As a matter of fact, yes," she says with a frozen smile, as if he'd asked her something else, like whether or not she parked in the faculty lot. Then her voice drops. "It *is* a fling. A very nice one."

Pictures of the two of them fill his head, Travis's soft, girlie hands on her gorgeous skin, on her curves, her full breasts. He blinks hard as if to erase them, and only feels more light-headed. "What about me?" he says, his voice too loud. The anger is in his throat. "Oh no, wait. It's too late, isn't it?" He turns to a wide-eyed family that's at the front of the line. "I'm completely and utterly screwed!" he says to them.

Margot stares at him, her lips pressed firmly together. She straightens. "Mr. Harrison," she says loudly, with all of her principal's authority, "don't make a scene." She turns her back and walks away.

Ned catches up to her in a shadowy space near the end of the stands. He grabs her wrist.

"Stop it," she says, trying to shake him off, but he grips her tighter. She turns her head to look for students and parents, but somehow, for just a moment, they are alone. In response to the P.A. announcer, one of the Corvettes on the field starts to honk its horn, and the crowd gives a roar. Margot puts her mouth in Ned's ear. "I don't know what your problem is, but you're making a fool of yourself. I'm going to kick you in your hurt knee. I'm not bluffing. Let go of me."

Her hot breath in his ear sends a shiver along the length of his body. Ned grabs her other forearm and tries to hold her. He wants to throw her to the ground and make love to her—he's filled with love and hate. They sway for a moment, her feet raising gray dust from the gravel. He can feel the tendons under her skin, elastic and hard as she pushes against him. He presses her arms back, until they are behind her waist and he has her in a bear hug He wants to keep squeezing until they both stop breathing, until they are both dead, as dead as his father.

He thinks for a moment that he won't let her go—that this time he will have her forever.

"Ned?" Margot says, her voice as small as a little girl's. "What's the matter with you?" She sounds like Ellie.

And then Ned feels his shoulders shaking. His arms loosen, and then he is crying, his face buried in her neck. But it doesn't seem like grief that he's feeling; it is almost a physical collapse, like something has failed inside of him.

"Just keeping you on your toes," he says, his hands still clasped around her, his voice muffled in her neck. "Not trying to hurt you." He takes in the apple smell of her skin and he wishes one big thing. He wishes he could say what he never did when they were together—that she was the most beautiful woman he'd ever known, and it frightened him, and he had hidden that fear, pretended that she wasn't enough for him, which wasn't true and which drove her away. It was the cruelest, most foolish thing he could have done. And even though he has married again and he loves Sally, he does so as a different sort of man, a man of deepest regret, who knows he could have loved Margot better.

He wants to touch Margot's face. But he doesn't.

"Your lips have gone pale," Margot says, managing to free a hand and press it against his chest, creating space between them. "And you're sweating terribly. You're not well, Ned." She extricates herself the rest of the way and smiles weakly at a trio of women who are approaching. "Everything's fine," she says, waving at them. She shrugs in an exaggerated, theatrical way. But Ned can hardly see them—as if they are only memories, people who exist in another time.

"Just keeping you on your toes," he says again. "I bet I gotcha."

Margot smiles more broadly now, almost like in the cafeteria. "You're sure a kidder," she says as she steps further back, her hands hovering in front of her, as if even in this apparent dénouement Ned might lunge out again.

But he turns away, doesn't wave at her over his shoulder, just limps back toward the open end of the fence. He can see her in his mind's eye getting smaller behind him, a beautiful dark-haired girl in green. It's done. He wipes at the sweat in his eyes, and he fumbles in his pocket for his cell phone. "I'm going to the hospital," he says to Sally's voicemail. "You were right, I'm not feeling too good." He tries to laugh. "You must be, like, a professional or something." Sally will meet him and Ellie there, he knows. She will be mad at him for being so stupid, for risking his health inexplicably, and later she'll forgive him, because she and Ned are too old not to forgive.

But for now, the crowd is cheering the return of the football team, as if the boys Mike Lester coaches are as great as any Ned's father drove to excellence, as if everything is new again, as if there is no score on the board.

LEAVING RENO

Fiona's fourteen-year-old son griped about the February weather for the entire thirty minutes they waited at BWI Airport for her mother to arrive. "It's a good thing you brought Grandma that sweater," he said. "She doesn't know what the word *sucks ass* means yet." He is tall, as tall as he is skinny, and his voice hasn't changed.

"That's two words," Fiona said, without looking up from *Condé Nast Traveler* magazine, and then she counted the words off on her fingers. "Sucks. Ass."

Jeremy shrank away from her as if she had a disease. "Whatever, math lady," he said.

Jeremy hated everything about Baltimore, or more specifically, the north corner of it where they now lived—in particular he disliked the wetness and the trees and the "redneck" quality of the people. What he did seem to enjoy was, first, being really angry with Fiona for moving them away from Reno and, second, serving up the word "ass" as if it were a tennis ball he could slice past her ear. Whiz. Booyah!

She believed, however, that Jeremy was observant enough to know that his grandfather was the true culprit. After a ten-year absence, Fiona's father, Charles Ray, had appeared at their front door and begun following them both all over town—to the mall, to work, to school, to Jack in the Box, even to friends' houses. He hadn't been dangerous. He just cowered in that beat-up Dodge Neon with the one silver door and pretended to read the *Reno Gazette-Journal*. But he'd been so relentless, sort of like one of those telemarketers, that Fiona finally packed a moving truck in the middle of the night. That had been six months ago.

Now, Fiona's mother Shirlene emerged from the airplane gate tentatively, moving slowly enough that she held other passengers back, like maybe she'd only half believed Baltimore existed. She scanned the crowd, waving like a beauty queen when she spotted Fiona and Jeremy waiting for her. She was as put together as ever—bright pink lips, a white top with a sparkly fish on it, pink pedal pushers, and strappy sandals that showed off her shapely feet. Jeremy sighed. "Grandma is so cool. Not like *some* people." He crossed his arms. "I'm not talking to you while she's here. Now I have someone else to talk to."

Fiona and Jeremy had been arguing for two days about whether or not it was dangerous for him to ride bikes with his friend Zack at the construction site down the street, zooming ten feet into the air from a concrete pipe. But even before that, it was hard for Fiona to remember their last good-natured or even neutral conversation. Since they'd moved from Nevada, Jeremy had regularly been skipping school and not doing his homework, and lately she'd had to pick him up at the Royal Farms convenience mart on her way home from work, learning from the assistant manager that he'd spent the whole day hanging out there at the edge of the parking lot with some derelict named Vlad. She reprimanded him, even yelled at him sometimes, but only because she knew she should, not because she felt the things it seemed like she was supposed to. Sometimes, she imagined herself giving up, the way a person might, in a moment of cerebral detachment, imagine letting their car drift over the side of a bridge.

"If you don't want to talk to me, then don't," she said. "I really don't care."

Letting his guard down, Jeremy made eye contact that showed hurt surprise. He looked, for a moment, hollow-eyed and quivering in the shoulders, like a young version of his grandfather, instead of like his regular fourteen-year-old self. On the one hand, Jeremy had recently stopped telling romantic stories about his grandfather—the ski bum, the man who once lived in a canoe for six months, the scalper at the Sundance Film Festival. On the other, once the man actually resurfaced and began disrupting their lives, it did seem that Jeremy had picked up Charles Ray's hang-dog expressions—the one Charles Ray displayed when Fiona said no, she definitely would not attend the father-daughter picnic at the Kiwanis Club; the one when she explained that leaving a Chihuahua puppy in the mailbox was pathological, not cute; the one when she threatened to turn him in to the sheriff for all of the bad checks he was writing to buy Jeremy butterfly knives and fireworks.

"Whatever," Jeremy said now, collecting himself. He sulked down into his oversized black jacket and slipped over to look out the big windows at the gray drizzle—leaving Fiona to greet her mother by herself. Reno, it was true, had 300 days of sunshine a year.

Shirlene was still, at fifty-eight, a cocktail waitress at the Golden Nugget. Even now, she walked with the hurried sashay of a glamorous casino girl, and the effect wasn't lost on a few of the businessmen waiting for their flights. Fiona wished, right then, just as she had when she was little, that she could hold on to who her mother was at that moment and keep her that way. Shirlene was like a comet, like something beautiful shooting through Fiona's life. That ephemeral magical quality always vanished the moment Shirlene opened her mouth.

"Sweetheart," Shirlene said, arms extended. Fiona reached out and held her mother, taking in the lean shape of her—like a greyhound. "Look at you," her mother said, pushing free. "You poor thing, you look awful."

At moments like this, Fiona remembered that comets were giant fireballs that could incinerate you on contact. She sighed, started to speak, then caught herself and smiled. "Yeah, I know," she finally said. She had been working overtime at the anachronistically-named Indian Summer Retirement Home, where she was a nurse's aid. Financing her night classes at the community college, along with her transfer fees from the nursing program in Nevada, had been more expensive than she'd anticipated.

But in the last month and a half, she had gotten through all of the hours of changing bedpans by thinking about what she'd written. Her essay was one of ten finalists in the "Plastics and Nursing" Essay Contest, sponsored by Plasticorps. Her achievement was why Shirlene had come to visit in the first place. It had been the perfect opportunity for Fiona to show Shirlene that the move was a good thing, that the distance could, in a strange way, make their little family more functional. That night, she and Shirlene and Jeremy would all go to the award ceremony, held at the Holiday Inn in Baltimore County, a fifteen-minute drive from Fiona's house. The three winners would receive scholarships that could be applied to a nursing degree at a real university. Fiona had always been a strong writer, and she thought her essay might just be unique enough to win; it was called "Will You Marry Me?" and she'd written it as a dialogue between a prosthesis and a truncated body part. She had worked to create something that she could imagine flowing from the pen of Caroline Parker, the RN at work that Fiona most admired, most wanted to be like—the way she glanced at patients' charts, instantly comprehending the secret language of medicine, her pretty dark head cocked to one side and her brow completely smooth. Unlike Fiona, who cinched up every muscle in her face when she pored over her medical books in the evenings, spinning them upside down in hopes that the molecule diagrams would suddenly make sense. One day, though, she would have those letters after her name—**R** (eal) **N** (urse).

"Where's Jeremy?" Shirlene said, but then she spotted his bulky coat over by a couple who were holding a baby up to the window and pointing at the airplanes. "Ah, he's dressed as a flasher for Halloween. In February." She smiled at Fiona. "Speaking of trick-or-treat, I've got a surprise for you two. I wonder what Jeremy will think."

"What is it?" Fiona said, reaching for the white shoulder bag at Shirlene's feet.

"I'm pretty sure you won't like it," Shirlene said, grinning in the same sugary way she had when Fiona came home from school one day to find that a doorman from Westward Ho! was now her fourth stepfather.

Fiona let go of the bag. "What is it?" she said with a feeling of dread, giving her mother her full attention now.

Shirlene reached out and tucked Fiona's limp damp hair behind her ear. Her voice dropped in volume and took on a grating tone intended to be soothing. "He promised he wouldn't bother you. No drinking. No groveling. And absolutely—he swore to me already—no boring skiing stories." Shirlene put her hands on Fiona's shoulders and looked at her right in the eyes. "Sweetheart, I really made him swear."

"Mom," Fiona said, an awful comprehension spreading through her chest, down her legs. "What have you done?" She turned around and scanned the sea of faces in the airport—young families, old couples, a woman with a barking terrier, a group of teenagers in marching band costumes.

Then she spotted Charles Ray lurking behind a souvenirs cart. He had on an Old Bay hat and sunglasses, the price tag still dangling over the bridge of his nose, but Fiona didn't know who he thought he was fooling. He stood over 6'5" and he had a ruddy complexion, red hair, and tattoos of birds all over his arms. Under one arm, he clutched a small crate with the Chihuahua in it. "Oh my God," Fiona said. She felt sick.

"Why can't you just try to get along with him?" Shirlene said. "You two should make up. And then you and Jeremy can come home."

"Are you out of your mind?" Fiona said. "This *is* home." Deep down, Fiona had long been vigilant for an excuse to move away from Nevada, and Charles Ray's return had made it easy. She had always wanted to be something more than a local girl with a notorious ski bum for a father and a mother who had made a profession of marrying charismatic drifters. It hadn't helped her image or her mobility when at twenty Fiona herself had become a widow with a child. What kind of fool actually married a rodeo cowboy? What Fiona wanted now were those two letters, **R** (eal) **N** (urse)—and once she had them, they would be a like a talisman that permitted only respectable behavior in herself and those around her.

She looked over now at Charles Ray, who seemed to be waiting for some kind of signal from Shirlene—as if Fiona couldn't plainly see him peeking over the rack of Ravens souvenir ties. He caught sight of Fiona and waved tentatively, wiggling his fingers.

"Not yet," Shirlene said in a stage whisper, gesturing for him to duck down.

Sometimes, Fiona thought now, it seemed like maybe Charles Ray and her mother were reverse talismans—things that warded off success. Even having picked up and left, it seemed like she might never escape Reno, never be an RN.

"Charles Ray is a people person," Shirlene said

brightly, "and he misses you more than you can imagine. Besides, all men need second chances from time to time."

"I'm not bringing him to my home," Fiona said. "And I would appreciate it if you would go and tell him that—discreetly. Jeremy doesn't need anymore upheaval right now."

"Sweetie—"

"Mother, bringing him here, not asking me, it's a breach of trust. That man stole all of the money out of my piggy bank."

Shirlene laughed. "It was such a long time ago. You did stupid things when you were younger, too."

"Do you know how much fifty dollars is to a nine year old?"

"You would have just frittered it away on horse books and those silly foreign stamps you liked to collect."

"Mom, Jeremy and I will be waiting for you in the car. Just you."

"Fiona!" her mother called after her. Then, in a sweeter voice, "Fi-fi. He's here now. Maybe you're upset, but at this point, where is he supposed to go?" Fiona closed her eyes for a moment. She kept walking, angling over toward Jeremy.

Shirlene appeared later from one of the doors marked Arrivals, where Fiona was waiting for her, the windshield wipers squeaking and tinny music escaping from Jeremy's headphones in the back seat. Fiona was so stunned by what her mother had done she couldn't feel anything, not even as she loaded the bags into the trunk, glancing nervously beyond the Arrivals sign—into the hulking masterpiece of space-aged architecture that was BWI Airport—and then drove away.

They didn't speak for most of the half-hour car ride to Fiona's house, north of the airport. Finally, Jeremy leaned forward between the seats and looked at them. "Dearest family of mine, what in the hell's going on?" he said.

"Watch your language," said Fiona. She glanced in the rearview mirror and caught sight of Jeremy's wrinkled forehead. He had always wrinkled it like that when he was confused, ever since he was blond-headed toddler. She felt herself softening. "Your grandmother and I don't agree about something. That's all."

"Yeah, well, no shit. That's as obvious as your ass in those Mom jeans," he said.

"He never used to talk like that," Shirlene said. She turned to look at him.

Fiona glanced in the rearview mirror, embarrassed. "What is the matter with you?" These weren't Mom jeans. Were they?

"Nothing's wrong with me. You guys are the ones with the problem." He sighed then and leaned back, pretending to look at the sparkly view of the stadium and the harbor from I-95. He did have a point, Fiona thought. She got onto I-83, driving past the familiar billboard for Utz Potato Chips and backs of colorful row houses, and then exited toward her neighborhood.

"He never had these problems before," Shirlene said, turning to Fiona.

"He wasn't fourteen before," Fiona responded, maybe too quickly. She tried to catch Jeremy's eye in the mirror so that she could glare at him, warn him to behave himself. Her mother was like a terrier; she would get on the scent and dig and dig and dig.

"Sweetheart," Shirlene said. "How can you cope on your own? I don't know if being out here by yourself is such a good idea."

"Look," Fiona snapped. "Don't pretend you want to help me. Bringing Charles Ray along, that was a purely selfish decision on your part."

"Bringing *who* along?" Jeremy said, leaning forward again, his eyes wide, his earphones around his neck. He clicked off his music.

"Nothing," said Fiona. "Forget it."

"I heard what you said. What's that slack-ass doing here? And where'd you put him?"

"Jeremy!" Shirlene said. "That's your grandfather you're talking about."

"I don't have a grandfather. I'm a bastard."

"What does that even mean?" Fiona said, laughing a bit too loudly, trying to act like this was just some schtick the two of them did.

"Jeremy Turner!" Shirlene said, her voice shaking. "You most certainly do have a grandfather. And he's come all this way to see you."

"Why?"

"Because he loves you. He wants to see you."

Fiona snorted. "Give me a break, Mom."

"Give me a break, Mom," Jeremy said, mocking. "I think I might use that one myself."

"God, will you please shut up!" Fiona said. "I'm sick to death of you."

Jeremy slumped back in the seat. "Bitch," he muttered.

"What?" Fiona said. "What?"

"You know what." Jeremy said, leaning forward again. "Anyhow, maybe I'd like to see old Gramps. Maybe I'd like to live with him instead of you."

Fiona clenched her jaw and pulled over to the side of the road, next to a garden center, decorative flags fluttering in front of it. Across the street was some kind of demolition site and evidence of preparations to build something new—enormous piles of gravel that seemed even duller in the gray mist of the afternoon. She yanked at the seat belt and turned around to look at him. "That's fine, then go. I can take us right back to the airport, right now. I'll give you the money for the ticket. Go live with your grandfather, who never gave two shits about whether we were alive or dead. Or, here's another choice— Go live with her," Fiona said, pointing at Shirlene, who looked on the verge of tears. "Here's the woman who loved you so much that she once drank herself unconscious while she was babysitting you. You were four fucking years old. Do you remember that? You remember when you woke her up and she puked in your hair?" She paused and looked at each of them. "How does that sound?"

"Fiona, sweetie," Shirlene said quietly, in almost a whisper.

Jeremy opened his car door. "I hate you," he said matter-of-factly. He jumped out and darted straight into traffic.

"Jeremy!" she shrieked.

Two cars skidded and barely missed him. Then he was in the construction site, running. Fiona saw him clearly for the first time in months, saw him for what he was—a child in baggy camouflage pants, all bony elbows and flapping legs, and a mess of blond hair. Right then, she loved him, almost as if her love was a coin, a quarter somewhere on those piles of gravel across the street, something gray and invisible except when the light hit it the right way. His thin arms pumping wildly, he ran faster than she imagined he could toward the woods at the other side of the site. And then he was gone.

Fiona buried her face in her hands. "Jesus," she said.

"Get out there, girl," Shirlene said. "There goes your son."

Fiona went over to the site, waded out into what she discovered was a muddy slog of weeds and dirt. How had he run in this? She called to him, and then she stood there by the side of the road for fifteen minutes. But Jeremy didn't come back. Fiona shook her head, felt her stomach turning, and crossed the road to her car. Neither she nor Shirlene uttered a word as she pulled away from the curb and continued toward home, another two miles away. Along Belvedere Avenue, the bony, naked pear trees were positioned like sentries; Fiona thought sadly about how much she already loved this place—the way there were four predictable seasons, and the buildings were older than she was, with bricks and cornices and dormer windows. When she was a child, she'd always imagined herself in an East-Coast family. She'd have brothers named Randall and James and a 100-year-old house covered in snow and Christmas lights. What Shirlene actually provided as a home was a ground floor apartment in a turquoise building and a chain-smoking babysitter next door, who'd named her twins after characters on *Days of Our Lives* and when that show was on would not permit Fiona or any of the other twenty children she watched to come indoors, not even in a *Washoe zephyr*, a severe Reno storm. Fiona gripped the steering wheel more tightly.

Four hours later, at six o'clock, Jeremy still hadn't turned up. Fiona phoned Zack and the rest of Jeremy's friends several times, but none of them claimed to know where he was. None of their parents answered the phone when she called, which made her feel even worse. All of these children could be lying to her.

"If he's not dead, I'm going to kill him," she said and slammed down the receiver. Then she picked up the phone and called the police, but after she explained the situation, they only took a description and told her to call back in a couple more hours. Officers would keep an eye out, but it wasn't considered an emergency just yet.

"Honey, he's just mad," Shirlene said. "Strong feelings like that always pass, even if you don't want them to. Nobody's stubborn enough to stay out in the woods when it gets cold at night."

Fiona had not even bothered to give Shirlene a quick tour of the small, old, wooden house she lived in now, nor had she let Shirlene have the master bedroom, her own room, like she had planned; the suitcases still lay in the middle of the living room floor. In her anger, her instinct for hospitality had left her as quickly as her mothering instincts. She had hardly spoken for the last several hours because she was afraid of what she might say to her mother, maybe something else that could never be taken back. She could not imagine the nurse she admired, Caroline Parker, having problems like this—Caroline Parker's parents were probably still together, her mother probably had beautifully manicured hands and a volunteer job reading to needy children, her voice smooth and rich like tiramisu. Her mother was probably someone who could be trusted with children. Caroline Parker was probably someone who could be trusted with children.

Shirlene sat on the sofa now, shivering in the sweater that Fiona had brought her. "Honey, why don't you go on to that awards ceremony?" she said. "I can stay here and wait for Jeremy to come home. If another hour and a half goes by, I can call the cops again for you."

"You're joking, right?" Fiona said.

"Honey," Shirlene said. "You need to stop thinking everything's about you. Anybody can wait for a kid who's probably just out throwing Coke bottles at train cars."

Fiona opened her mouth, felt anger rising in her chest. She paused. Maybe it would be good if she went away for a little while and cooled down. She needed to figure out what to do, not just about Jeremy but also about Charles Ray. Her mother wouldn't say where he'd gone, but, much to Fiona's frustration, she had apparently told him to find a phone somewhere and call Shirlene's cell later in the evening. Charles Ray didn't believe in cell phones, but Fiona knew that just meant he couldn't afford one.

She needed to collect herself, get logical. That wasn't easy because every time she looked at her mother, her face got hot. "You'd phone me the moment Jeremy came back?" Fiona said, waving her own cell phone.

Shirlene nodded. "I know how those things work," she said.

"And if he's not back by eight, you'll call me and the police? I'll come right away."

"Yes."

"And of course, it goes without saying that you will not give Charles Ray any information whatsoever. Not about where this house is, not about Jeremy. Nothing."

"You know, sweetie, I'd hoped he could tell you this himself, but Charles Ray has joined GIVE. It's like a twelve-step program for selfish people. He says he understands why you don't trust him, but he's just got to keep giving until he finds something you're willing to receive."

Fiona only stared at her mother. It was an act of will to keep her mouth shut.

"Fine, fine. Of course," Shirlene said brightly. "You go and have fun. Jeremy's just being a boy. I know things will turn out just fine."

Without changing clothes or even looking at her lank hair, Fiona got in the car and drove around her neighborhood, checking all of Jeremy's favorite haunts—the construction sites, the Royal Farms, the McDonald's parking lot. When she drove to the Holiday Inn where the awards evening had been underway for over an hour, she hesitated and then pulled in. She sat in the car with her eyes closed for five minutes, thinking how much this night had meant to her—more than she had even realized. In retrospect, she could see that she'd thought the awards ceremony would help Jeremy understand what she'd been working for. Even if she didn't win, she was a finalist, and he could get a sense of her dedication and the respect her colleagues gave her. But not tonight. She grabbed her purse and got out of the car. The dark sky was low and hazy, a buffer between herself and the wide piercing stare of the moon, a stare that had filled her window every night of her lonely childhood in Reno. She liked the way the dampness here hugged the green light of the Holiday Inn sign, making everything seem smaller somehow, more manageable. She wouldn't stay long, she told herself, just a few minutes, long enough to tell someone in charge that she was grateful, but there was a family matter she had to address.

Inside the red ballroom were about twenty round tables and a rectangular head table for the speakers. There was a buffet dinner and men in rigid white chefs' hats were serving roast beef to people in suits and nice velvet dresses, who were lined up with plates in hand. The hostess checked Fiona's name off the list. "No guests?" she said in a bubbly way, smiling sympathetically. Fiona felt her jaw set when she thought about the expensive tickets. She thought back to the soaring feeling she'd when she picked them up, wanting to shake the woman that she was that day: *We are not normal people who wear velvet and eat roast beef!*

"No," Fiona said to the hostess and then she fought the urge to tell the whole story to her, to this stranger. Why did it matter what this girl thought? So what if Fiona was the only person to show up by herself. It didn't mean that no one cared about her. Did it? "They couldn't make it, after all," she said.

Fiona got seated at a small table with an oncologist from Greater Baltimore Medical Center. His niece, who was small and heavyset, was a finalist. The niece had asked him to be her date because her husband was in South America on a charity mission, giving vaccinations to the needy. "I talked to him on the phone tonight and he was exhausted," the niece said. Her name was Samantha and she wore a shiny pink dress and a string of pearls. Fiona suddenly felt self-conscious about her old chinos and gray sweater; the lipstick she'd put on in the restroom wasn't enough to help. "But he was so happy," Samantha continued. "They helped a lot of people."

"These two want to quit their jobs and join the Peace Corps," said the oncologist, whose name was Terry Feiffer. "As if this business her husband's doing isn't enough already. I think they're just trying to get away from my sister's cooking." He patted his small paunch. Their whole family was from Baltimore, for generations. Sometimes they left, but they always came back. "We must be gluttons for punishment."

"Speak for yourself," said Samantha, touching Terry's arm.

Fiona admired their playfulness. With her and her mother, talk was always serious. If one person needled another, it usually turned into an argument.

When Terry smiled, there was a gap between his teeth like the one David Letterman had, which made his jokes funnier. *I'll just sit here for a minute.* Fiona found herself laughing. But then she remembered Jeremy again and stopped herself. When was the last time someone had been able to make her laugh when she'd felt this bad? She thought about the one boyfriend she'd had since her husband had died eleven years ago—Daniel. He'd always been able to make her laugh. She remembered the funniest things he used to say her when they were lying together in bed. "You're my little lima bean," he'd say. "You're my little woodchuck, my little Tinker Toy." They would look at each other and crack up. But later, when things got more serious between them, he became distant. Until finally, three years ago, he disappeared all together.

"So anyway," Terry was saying. Only when she noticed they were both looking at her awkwardly did she realize that she had fallen silent.

Samantha pushed back from the table. "I'm just going to run to the ladies room. I'm so nervous I'm afraid I might burst. Not that I'm going to win or anything. I'm just nervous about having my name called. What if I miss it?"

After she left, Fiona turned to Terry, and as he

spoke she studied his broad nose, the astonishing darkness of his hair. She felt guilty for finding him attractive. For one thing, she knew she should be thinking only of Jeremy. She shouldn't even be here. For another, what was the point of thinking of a man? Terry caught her looking and he smiled awkwardly.

"I'm sorry," she said and paused, searching for more words. "I'm a little off tonight." She hesitated, but he had such a kind face. She found herself telling him about her mother and Charles Ray, and about Jeremy running away. Terry nodded thoughtfully as she spoke. When she finished, she brightened up a little. "Thanks," she said. "I think I just needed to tell someone that."

"No problem," he said. "I know it's no consolation right now, but an awful lot of boys go through periods like this." Then, he leaned forward. "Have you ever considered talking to your dad?"

"Why would I? He isn't the kind to help me with my son. For my fourteenth birthday, he mailed me some of those airplane bottles of bourbon. Who does that?"

"Yikes," Terry said.

Hearing those empathetic words, Fiona felt a little better, laughing more at his jokes and even making a couple of her own. Even so, she couldn't stop looking at her watch or wondering if Jeremy was okay. What if a tree branch fell on him in the woods, or, if he wandered through town and came across some weirdos in a public restroom? Part of her hated him for making her feel like this—ineffectual in her mothering, and worried almost beyond rationality. And then another part hated herself for hating him. She wanted to be like one of those more worthy worried mothers in a film—someone with big eyes and a handkerchief, someone who deserved for everything to be okay even if it wasn't.

At seven thirty, as the dinner plates were being taken from the tables, her phone rang. "Hi, it's me,"

Shirlene said. "Zack's mother called. She spotted Jeremy at Domino's. But she couldn't get him to come close enough to talk to."

"Okay," Fiona said, thinking things over.

"What do you want to do?" Shirlene said.

Fiona sighed. She thought things through. "Just tell the officers what you told me."

"Sure, Sweetie. Sure," said Shirlene. "Are you okay?" Her mother sounded soft then, like she really cared, like she was almost someone Fiona could count on.

"I think so," Fiona said, feeling as though she might cry. But then she thought about Charles Ray. "Mom? You haven't heard from You-Know-Who, have you?"

"No, and frankly I'm a little worried," Shirlene said. "I thought by now I'd have heard from him."

"Well, I'm not surprised," said Fiona, her face getting hot again. "If there's one thing that every man in our family does—" She caught herself, smiled at Terry, and said into the phone, "I've got to go, Mom. Call the station. And then call me back. I'll talk to you later." She hung up and put the phone back in her purse. Grudgingly, she admitted to herself that she could count on Shirlene when the chips were really down. Once, in the first grade, a teenaged neighbor boy had led Fiona away from the playground by the hand. Behind some trees, he pushed her down, reached under her dress, and pulled down her underpants. Over his shoulder, Shirlene appeared with a two-by-four raised over her head. Fiona had not even known that Shirlene was home or sober. She shut her eyes when the board struck the boy's head. She remembered Shirlene saying to the groaning, bloodied teenager, "Now you go figure out what lie you're going to tell your mama about where that came from." She and Shirlene had never spoken about the incident, not that day, not ever.

"Everything okay?" said Terry.

"No," Fiona said, smiling. "Not really. Though I can imagine it getting worse." She told herself she would only stay a little longer, but she felt anchored to her seat, like she was made of cement. She really did not want to face what was on the other side of those glass doors.

About fifteen minutes later, after a short speech from a Plasticorps representative and a professor from the community college, a man with very large glasses came to the mic to read out the three winners. The first name was Samantha's, as Fiona had expected. Samantha squeezed Terry and went to the head table. Then there was another name, and a woman across the room squealed. Fiona closed her eyes and concentrated on not being disappointed; there were some cash prizes for the runners-up, and anything would help. But then she heard the man saying her name, "Fiona Turner." *That's me*, she thought. *Isn't it?* She wasn't sure, even though it was the same name she'd had for the last thirteen years. She had simply never imagined it being spoken out loud at a moment like this. "Oh my God," she said slowly. "I'm Fiona."

After the presentations were over, they returned to their seats, Samantha bouncing ahead of Fiona and the other woman. Fiona was about to take her purse from the chair and go, when the hostess came to the table with three freshly corked bottles of champagne. "With compliments, Hon," she said, gesturing to Fiona and Samantha. Then, she winked at Terry, "I snuck you one, too." Fiona felt a little pang of jealousy and she imagined with pleasure Jeremy's mocking voice: *Hon*. Jeremy was right—it did sound stupid. She sat back down.

Much to Fiona's surprise, Caroline Parker appeared at their table then. "I just wanted to congratulate you," she said, leaning down to hug Fiona. Then she spotted Fiona's companions. "Hey, Terry!" She leaned down and kissed his cheek. "I heard about that McCarthy award. Wow, check you three out. This must be the A-list table." She turned to Terry. "I'm having lunch with your sister next week, so I'll get to hear all about your big event." Then she waved and she was gone again, as quickly as she had appeared.

For a few minutes then, even after Caroline was visible nowhere in the room, Fiona could hardly speak. And after that, she could hardly stop looking at Terry.

"Okay girls," Terry said, filling the glasses with free champagne. "They're going to kick us out of here before too long. So we have a lot of toasting to do in not much time."

"Well, okay," Fiona managed to get out. "Just a glass."

They raised their glasses. "To us," said Samantha.

"To us," Fiona repeated. And it felt good to say it, to congratulate herself for something well done.

Pretty soon, the champagne was all gone. They were all going in the same direction, so they only ordered one taxi and they dashed from the warm lobby when it arrived, piling in one after the other. When they stopped in front of Samantha's house a short while later, Fiona thought that it looked like the kind of place someone might call a bungalow. There were window boxes that would undoubtedly bloom in spring and there was a porch swing. "We must get together and talk about the future," Samantha said, reaching across Terry to grip Fiona's hands in hers. "Promise?"

"You're slurring," said Terry. "Go to bed."

"Okay, okay," Samantha said. She turned to Fiona. "Talk to you soon." Outside the taxi, she shouted at the night sky, "Plastic!"

Fiona and Terry watched Samantha's broad form weave up the front steps. She dropped her house keys several times before disappearing into the house with a final *Beverly Hillbillies* wave. When the cab pulled away again, Fiona and Terry both sighed and leaned back. Fiona held closer the winner's plaque and envelope she'd been given. "Who'd have thought that could happen at a Holiday Inn?" Terry said. "What a night, huh?"

"You have no idea," said Fiona, turning her head and smiling at him.

"Come here," he said and draped his arm over her shoulder. The sudden weight of it there startled her. Her breath quickened. She thought for a moment that she might cry. The streetlights washed over the two of them, casting dull yellow light. After a few minutes, rain began to fall on the roof of the car.

"Hey Driver," said Terry. "Go down Belvedere, would you? Drive us past the Domino's, the McDonald's, and the Royal Farms. Slowly." He glanced at Fiona. "I'll pay extra."

There was no sign of Jeremy in any of the parking lots, and when she called the police, the officer said they had dispatched a description and had issued an amber alert. Her best course of action was to wait at home.

When they arrived there, Fiona saw it as if for the first time, as if she were Terry—the loose rain gutter and the chipping white paint and the hole in the screen door. She looked at the dark windows and then at Jeremy's bicycle sprawled in the middle of the yard and she thought maybe she would not be able to leave the cab. Maybe she could pretend she'd made a mistake about her address. Maybe she would make the driver take her somewhere else, anywhere else. Once inside, she would have to deal with her mother, or get in a shouting match with Jeremy—if he were there.

Instead, she found herself saying, "Will you come in for a minute? We can just call another cab when we're ready."

Oh God, no, she thought, *What am I doing?*

But when she heard Terry saying, "Okay," and following her out of the car, she felt strangely relieved.

They paid the cab driver and then, after she had peeked through the front window curtains, Fiona explained to Terry that they would have to tiptoe through the house because Shirlene was sleeping, and he would have to leave within a short time.

"Too bad I didn't bring my climbing gear. I could have dropped out the window," he said. Then he smiled and squeezed her hand. "Don't worry. I understand."

They took off their shoes and stole past Shirlene on the fold-out sofa. They creaked on the stairs but Shirlene still snored softly behind them, so they continued on. Upstairs, Fiona went into Jeremy's room and looked at his unmade bed. He had never been away from home at night before, not like this. She felt a weakness in her stomach, her legs—like she might kneel down by his bed and pray. But she thought if she did she might not be able to get up. She took a long look at his clothes on the floor, his hamster Marilyn running in its wheel, the dark, angry posters on the wall. He was becoming exactly the teenage boy she had always feared he might be. Then she closed his door gently behind her and went back in the hall, where Terry was waiting. She gestured to her own room, which was across from Jeremy's.

Once inside with the door shut, she flipped on the light and collapsed on the bed. "Oh God," she said. "This night is too hard. And I'm definitely drunk."

"Me, too," he said, standing stiffly near the door, hands in his pockets. "Well, it looks like the coast is clear."

"Yeah, I think it's safe. At least from the Charles Ray perspective. Thank you."

"You sure you're going to be okay?"

"I hope so," she said, patting the edge of the bed beside her. "Come sit down for a minute." He came over and sat down; she couldn't see his face. She reached up and began stroking his back.

He turned to look at her, his lips a pale thin line.

In the lamplight, she could see some small acne scars on his face. He opened his mouth, took a moment to speak. "It looks like things are all right, so maybe I should—"

At this moment, Fiona knew what he was going to say, could feel the way she would feel if he left— her raw exposure to the emptiness of the house, to the cloying familiarity of her own breath. She knew he wasn't comfortable there with her. But before she thought about what she was doing, she lunged toward him and kissed him passionately. She did not want to hear the end of the statement he'd begun. What she wanted was to kiss him deeply, almost pull him into her, let him occupy her.

He didn't push her away. They kissed for a few minutes, and then she moved to his neck. "Wow," he said breathlessly.

"Yeah, I know," she said, kissing his collarbone. "Wow."

"I haven't, you know, done this in a long time," he said.

"I haven't in a long time either," she said.

They looked at each other for a moment and then began hurriedly to remove one another's clothes— shirts, pants, socks, underwear. She touched Terry's hands, his thick hair, the skin on his elbows. She held him to her, gripping his wide-set shoulder blades. Terry's touch on her skin was both startling and comfortable.

When they were under the covers, with their bodies disappearing into one another, Fiona found herself thinking about the amputated body part in her essay, something suddenly made whole again. She could picture Caroline Parker's hands manipulating the smooth human nub into the plastic socket, the straps, the virtually seamless line. She could feel herself filling with emotion, she wasn't even sure what kind, as if Terry had pressed somewhere on her skin and released it. It came into her throat and tears began to stream down her face. She buried her face in his neck and he held her.

At 6 a.m., Fiona woke with a start and began getting Terry ready to leave. She called for a cab and crept into the hall holding Terry's hand. Even though she was a little hung over, Fiona couldn't remember when she'd felt so awake. They glanced in at Jeremy's room and found it still empty. At the bottom of the stairs, she took in her living room—watercolors of ducks, small round coffee table, plain white lamps. Even her sofas, which were a muted gold, looked as though they had come from a motel.

It was then, in the softening dark of morning that she saw, on the other sofa, a long red-haired lump under her favorite afghan, feet and gangly ankles sticking out. Charles Ray. She gasped. That little dog was even wedged under his armpit, asleep on its back.

"What's wrong?" Terry whispered.

This was Shirlene's doing. Fiona thought about shrieking at the top of her lungs and waking everyone and throwing him out of her house, out of her life for good this time. But then in a long slow moment, Charles Ray woke up and looked at her. She stared at his big light eyes that were just like Jeremy's, the fine lines of his forehead, the quizzical upturn of his wind-burned lips. He looked right at her, right into her eyes and she could feel a kind of love, a genuine uncomplicated fondness of the sort she had always imagined was reserved for the likes of Caroline Parker or for Samantha, not for her. Then he closed his eyes, pretending to be asleep, perfectly still under the blanket like he was dead. In his own way, he was actually trying to be cooperative, she thought, by not calling attention to himself, not making more complicated this moment she was having with Terry, a moment she did not know how to understand, a moment Charles Ray and Shirlene might have had themselves once upon a time.

"What is it?" Terry said, his hands on her shoulders. Somehow he had not noticed Charles Ray lying there.

Fiona opened her mouth, but nothing angry came out. She realized then how accustomed she was to that particular feeling. "It's nothing," she said. "I stepped on something sharp."

She showed Terry to the door and stood on the front stoop in her robe, shivering. The sun burned gray light behind the clouds and lit up the silent houses across the street. *The Baltimore Sun* hadn't even shown up yet.

Terry slipped his card into her hand. "Don't feel like you have to call. I don't want to lay anything heavy on you." He looked away for a moment and then back at her again.

"Yeah," she said, pulling her robe tighter. "It's fine, you know, if this isn't a big deal." She tried not to look at his dark eyes or the gap between his teeth.

"You know, we had a lot of fun last night. Is it really fine not to think about it?"

"Well, I don't know."

"What you mean is it'll be fine in the sense that it will be one of those 'character building' experiences, which usually means being miserable. Is that the kind of fine you mean?"

"Yes, that's the one," she laughed. God he was cute.

The cab pulled up just then. "Keep me posted about Jeremy, okay? Call me when he comes home." He grabbed her and kissed her and then he ran down to the car. She waved and then she came back inside to the kitchen to wait alone.

Later, after the newspaper arrived, Shirlene came into the kitchen humming "Some Enchanted Evening." She was looking at Fiona in a very pointed way. Fiona glanced back at her, annoyed. This was not Reno, and Terry had not been like the drifter cowboys who made one-night appearances in that turquoise apartment building. Had he? It occurred to Fiona then that she had no idea what had transpired between Shirlene and her boyfriends behind closed doors, any more than her mother could understand what had passed between her and Terry last night. Shirlene stopped humming when she saw Fiona's face. Then she began making coffee and toast. "Well, what happened?" she said.

"I won, if that's what you mean."

"Oh sweetie!" Shirlene said. "I told you everything would turn out fine. The thing about bad luck is that it doesn't last forever."

Fiona disagreed. She didn't believe in bad luck, just bad judgment, which was something that could be permanent, even fatal. But maybe, she had to admit, it was possible to go too far the other way, to paralyze yourself trying to avoid the lifetime of bad judgment you'd witnessed in your mother.

"I was thinking," Fiona said. "You could tell Charles Ray that if he gets a job and somewhere to live, if he's not a danger just by being who he is, I'll think about sending Jeremy back to Reno for part of next summer. He'd stay with you, though, of course."

"Of course," Shirlene said. They had their backs to each other, Fiona bent over the newspaper and Shirlene at the counter pouring coffee. "If Charles Ray had gotten this bug in his ear earlier," Shirlene said, "he might have made a decent father."

"Well," Fiona said and then she turned around to look at Shirlene. "He's still going to have to leave."

"Mmm," Shirlene said, sipping her coffee and conceding with a nod.

Fiona turned back to her paper and began to read, though her eyes were just scanning over the words. After a while, she heard the rattle of Jeremy's bicycle. For half a second, she didn't know what she was supposed to do, and then she hurried to the window, just in time to see him picking it up and walking it toward the road, giving a furtive glance at the window where Fiona stood.

She ducked a little and then she could hear him clear his throat, his voice still a boy's, still high-pitched. Then he sniffled, and she could just hear him fiddling with the kick stand, his nimble small hands very quick and quiet. These sounds were so familiar they were like part of her—her feet, her hands, her voice. In another family, with another mother, she thought, the child would be coming inside, or the mother would be rushing outside. But they didn't have that kind of closeness. Still, she thought, he wants me to hear. He kept fiddling, shaking the chain and padlock that hung loose over the handlebars. He didn't immediately pedal away and disappear into one of the dirt trails that veined the neighborhood. She went over to the window and let him see her, pretending to wash a cup in the sink, pretending not to notice the way his hair stood up in horns or the mud stains on his knees, pretending to look up and see him for the first time.

SHOW OF FORCE

Franz pulled onto Route 29, gestured to the empty road ahead. "See? We'll be fine without your mother." He scrutinized his son's profile, the outline of that new Adam's apple. Franz's secret didn't make his hands shake the way he almost wished.

Route 29 sliced through Maryland forest, trees cordoned by guard rails. Franz pointed at a bullet hole in the *Welcome to Clarksville* sign. "Check it out." His foot eased off the gas. They'd only lived out this way for nine months, and people who shot at signs still baffled him, as did the statuettes of crying Indians at Big Pat's Granite Ranch and the deer that milled in their yard, south of Baltimore, like it was a petting zoo.

He swerved over, hopped out onto glass and bottle caps. He plucked shell casings from the gravel, the way he'd been doing lately. His wife needed something, maybe a hobby. She could make shit out of these exploded bullets. Jewelry or whatever.

Rory leaned his head out the window. "Come on, Clutch. Stick to the mission." *Clutch* was military slang for a transport driver. Franz knew this because *Firestorm3*, a game about warfare in a fictional Mideast town, had been the screaming and exploding soundtrack of their lives for years. Today was the championship of the *Firestorm3* video game tournament, and Rory was at the top of the leader board. Or actually, Rory's alter ego, RekonDog, was at the top.

Franz glanced at his watch. His wife always allowed too much time for the suburban outposts further south, where the road widened to four lanes, the foliage cracked open to sky and quickie marts, and DC traffic slowed to a crawl. She'd become cautious in ways he didn't recognize. Maybe she'd infected Rory with it. Franz got back in the car. "Is that your signature cause, Miss America? Punctuality?"

"Listen, new guy." Rory pressed a finger to his lips. "Strictly tango uniform during the transport." *Tango uniform* meant *tits up*, which meant *dead*—which meant *no talking*. Rory, who was fourteen, returned to the message he was composing, probably to his coach, HotCross, a 21-year-old guru out west someplace. Recently, RekonDog had become something like a semi-professional athlete in the *Firestorm3* world—with sponsors, a coach, and a group of skinny, long-limbed teen fans enthralled by Rory's bad-boy tendency to throw equipment and mouth off at officials.

Franz had insisted on driving him to this last day of the competition, in spite of both his wife and his son's protests. Babette had even left him a note, scrawled on a paper plate that said, *This will be a big day for RD. He needs someone who knows where to park and which gear to hand him during play. No offense, but do you even know what a macro button looks like?* Underneath his wife's scrawl, Rory had written *Word!* in black marker and underlined it three times. He loved them, but they could go fuck themselves.

He decelerated by another ten miles an hour, glancing at Rory, who didn't look up from his phone. "Real mature," the boy muttered.

He did want to needle Rory, but he also wanted to stretch out the journey. He hadn't worked up to his big announcement. Franz had already signed a contract for a job in Texas, and he had done it without any discussion with either of them. Maybe it would be the right kind of jolt. Like that machine with the paddles that brought people back to life.

Babette took the boy to tournaments in Dallas every month. This move would put them closer to the action. Franz would be the guy who fulfilled his son's dreams, the guy who paid better attention than they gave him credit for. Maybe a few months would find the three of them in a Dallas art cinema at some old kung fu movie, himself in the middle holding the popcorn, all of them happily eating out of the tub.

Rory began some strange breathing exercises, a series of sharp gasps, and he seemed to study Clarksville as it passed—the Dairy Queen where Babette ate nonfat ice cream even though she'd lost so much weight and the St. Louis Parrish Church that had been here since 1855 and that, as atheists, they would never attend.

They'd moved up here after Babette lost her long-time job as a bicycle messenger in DC—she'd been attacked by two men in broad daylight. After they wrestled her to the ground, one man held her down while the second one grabbed her belongings, including the client's package, and rode away on her expensive bicycle. What had haunted her, what made it impossible to go back, she whispered to him once after waking from one of her pre-dawn nightmares, wasn't the men who'd robbed her—who were just desperate and poor. Rather, it was the blank stares of the suit-wearing assholes who hadn't stopped to help.

Nowadays, when he got home at around eight or nine, he found Babette and Rory in the living room, his son playing *Firestorm3* and shouting obscenities, his wife watching from behind the couch, cheering his sniper shots, ducking as if bullets might whiz from the giant screen. From the back, their blond heads made them twins. Franz snuck through the living room and hurried upstairs, where he took a shower and masturbated and then read a book. He hated the way they looked at him if he dared to initiate, say, a *conversation* while Rory played that goddamn game. But it didn't mean he was a misanthrope, as Babette liked to claim.

Today the two of them would finally get that. Fluffy clouds drifted in the June sky above the treetops. The sun warmed the beige interior of the car, and the tires created a hum. When they heard the news, would they carry him around the living room on their shoulders, like a sports hero?

"That weird face you're making is distracting. I'm trying to get my Zen on." Rory said. He still gazed out the window. The boy had heightened senses, could see Franz even when he wasn't looking. "Mom was right," Rory said. "If I take your ignorance of my process personally, I'll only hurt myself."

"Your process?" Franz laughed. She said that? He reached over like he might pick Rory's nose, but Rory shrank from his hand like a martial arts expert. Those reflexes—the kid never missed a trick. Rory was famous for combat techniques like "show of force" which involved dropping harmless flares to lure the enemy, and then annihilating him before he knew what happened.

"You're still doing it," Rory said. "Stop."

"This is just my *face*," said Franz. His neck flushed warm.

"If I'm not mistaken, you're still talking."

"How are you feeling about the competition today?" A cloud had drifted over the sun, and the wall of trees on either side cast a dark, almost wet shadow over the car. He didn't have to squint at his son, whose body filled the passenger seat the way an adult's would. That was new.

Rory scooted up straight. Franz could only glance

at him in snapshots, because of the way the road twisted through the forest now. Rory studied the bend ahead with wild eyes. "It's about stats. Not feelings," he said. "The stats show I'll kick everyone's ass in this Podunk contest and then go to nationals to kick ass in Dallas. Yet again." Rory wasn't exaggerating about his odds. His college fund was nearly as big as Franz's retirement portfolio.

But feelings didn't factor? Rory kept getting suspended from school. He was the kind of boy who was always going to lose his shit when his friends made remarks about Babette, with her low-cut fishnet tops and the opium flower tattoo on top of her breast. She was the same petite blond she'd been in high school—the one who'd hitchhiked to the punk rock show where Franz had met her. Not the first girl with whom he'd smoked weed in the alley behind the club. Not the first with whom he'd had sex in his parked car. But the only one who'd made him laugh, who seemed to find it fun, rather than like she was proving something to someone who wasn't even there.

"And then what?" said Franz. "Let's say you win all of the money and whatnot. What happens next?" He waited for Rory to say something about Dallas, about how tired he was of airplanes, maybe even how awesome it would be to live there.

"I'm the champion of the whole country. I've got an ATV and ten grand and, as of next year, a learner's permit." He leaned forward, making sharp, angry gestures with his hands. "What happens is I go to Korea for the World Cyber Games. Mom's talking home schooling! She says we're moving to Vegas!" He laughed and put his hand up for a high five. "I'm going to be the Tony Hawk of *Firestorm3*."

The 1980's Tony Hawk reference, he knew, had been for his benefit. And some distant part of him, in a windy backwater of his brain, knew the high five was a *monumental* gesture from Rory. But he was too stunned to return it. Korea? Vegas? Home schooling?

Why hadn't Babette mentioned any of this? He touched his forehead, cold from the air conditioner.

Franz turned toward Rory, started to speak, and then hesitated. "But I thought everything happens in Dallas?"

Rory sighed, put his hand down. "Please. The international action is in Vegas."

Franz could feel the color drain from his face. He re-lived the spectacular way he'd quit his job last week. His firm was defending a pharmaceuticals giant called Pro-Concepts, which had used a toxic ingredient in pediatric epilepsy medication. Franz's job for the past year consisted of combing through emails until late at night. In a meeting, amped on energy drinks, he heard himself say to his firm's partners, "We might *win* this case?" He pointed at the suits from Pro-Concepts, guys wearing Armani and big watches. "You people butt-fucked a bunch of kids." He already had a new job, so what the hell.

A few people—mostly fellow low-ranking lawyers —congratulated him later, while he packed his things, as if he were a vigilante. But he'd made plenty of money working this shitty case. And a lot of other shitty cases. If anyone was a dick, it was Franz. At least these other guys believed in what they were doing.

Still, maybe he'd been hasty. The papers he'd signed with the firm in Texas made his chest contort. If there was one thing you didn't want to do with a bunch of lawyers, it was break a contract.

Franz's accelerator foot pressed heavy, numb. They'd reached the spot where the road widened, but hadn't caught up to the suburban traffic. The engine whined. Rory folded his arms across his chest. "What now, *Francis*," he said.

The boy had taken to using "Francis," which was Franz's given name, instead of "Dad." He could have at least used "Franz," the name that friends had christened him in high school. The guys in his band decided that "Franz" was a tougher name than "Francis," maybe because it was German—something appropriate for a big, broad-chested punk rock guitarist, a guy getting straight A's on a dare, a guy who the principal called to the cafeteria a few times to settle disputes like a bouncer.

Maybe Rory's insistence on "Francis" was retaliation for the fact that Franz still called him *Rory* instead of *RekonDog* or *RD*.

Franz took a deep breath. Surely, Dallas was more relevant to Rory than DC?

A moving company had to be contracted by next week if they were going to make it down there when the job started. The new firm did represent corporate clients. He still wasn't a public defender like he's always said he'd be, sticking up for the poor. But on the other hand, Franz would be an associate and not just some research monkey. He'd be able to afford for Babette to stay home and for Rory to go to college.

Rory wouldn't find these details compelling, but maybe he'd find them reasonable. "*RD*," he said. He wasn't sure how to introduce the topic. "Sometimes your mother and I make choices—I mean, we do things and they affect your life."

"Mom already told me that boring story about how you met, if that's what you're about to tell me," he said, cutting Franz off in a flat monotone. "The Razor Club." He rolled his eyes and used finger quotes.

Franz stopped short. "When did you find out about that?"

Rory shrugged.

How much had she told him? A fluttering sensation grew in his chest. Was there a chance that she still thought about that night, about the way they'd thrust against the back window of his VW, the way he'd broken up a fight later and she'd slipped him her number? He experienced a slight tingling in his crotch like he might get an erection. Jesus. He wished he could be the person he'd been back then, the person you wanted behind you if there was trouble —instead of the irrelevant man who combed through emails in an office while his wife was robbed.

"Are you crying?" Rory said now, his nose wrinkled in that same disgusted way as when Franz tried to get him to use Febreze in his room. Babette never went in there because she said it was Rory's "personal space," and as a result, the room reeked like old cheese.

Rory laughed into his hand. "Good thing you don't still wear *eyeliner*."

"Eyeliner was a counter-cultural *statement*." Franz wiped his face. There was no one *crying* in this car. He glanced over at Rory, who studied him as if his entrails were spilling out over the belt of his pants.

God, he was tired of that look. "I was just thinking," he said. "The night I met your mother a band called R.I.P. played a song called 'I Fucked Your Mother.'" He felt the hot urge to reach for Rory's throat. Instead, he said, smiling, "And it's true. I *did* fuck your mother." He laughed.

They stared at each other for a moment, and Franz regretted what he'd said, not least because it wasn't how he felt about that night. The trees had begun to fall away to wide gravel shoulders and strip malls. They passed a chainsaw sculpture of a bear outside a Shell station.

"Listen—" he started to say. But he didn't get the chance to finish.

Despite the impossibility of the angle, somehow Rory managed to lurch across from the passenger seat and punch Franz. Hard. Franz's head hit the driver's side window. He lost control of the car and swerved across the double yellow line for a moment, cars honking and driving onto the shoulder.

After he regained control and got back into his lane, Franz pulled to the side. "Get out of the car." He barely knew what he was saying.

The boy stared straight ahead for a moment, not moving. "Get out!" Franz shouted.

Rory opened the car door, let it swing wide. He got out, one slow, deliberate foot at a time. Afterward, he turned and pulled his cell phone from his front pocket, wiggling it for Franz to see—as if he were the parent, as if he were the one teaching Franz a hard lesson. "I have one of these," he said. Then he gestured to Rt. 29, straight and wide to the horizon, a litter of auto body shops and drycleaners and fried chicken. "And I'm on a mobility corridor." It was military lingo for "a well-traveled road." Franz could see in the boy's eyes something he could not quite place, something he hoped was fear. As soon as the door slammed shut, Franz pressed the accelerator to the floor, trying to spray Rory with gravel, though the Nissan engine wasn't powerful enough for that.

He turned around and Rory gave him the finger as he passed. He drove south on the highway, refusing to allow himself to check on the lanky boy in the rearview mirror. Hadn't there been a time when they used to draw pictures together, the boy's wrists so impossibly tiny, his cloud of blond hair so like his own in childhood photos? He drove for five miles, back through Clarksville.

When they had moved here nine months ago, Rory had been all bony knees and elbows. He still looked enough like that child he'd once been that they could convince themselves they were getting their suburban house and yard for him—they weren't fleeing the city or what happened. They just wanted to live in a big old house, something with character.

Soon, he drove out the other side of the town and found himself in pristine Maryland second-growth forest. He passed their street. When he got to the Battlefield Days Inn, he swerved into the lot. It was an old salmon-colored place, with external walkways on all three floors. He booked himself into a room, even though it was only three in the afternoon.

He gathered ice from the machine down the hall, and then he went back to the room and shoveled handfuls of it into one of his socks. He lay on the bed, sock pressed to his jaw. All those fights had taught Rory how to punch, that was one thing he could say.

He had left his son. He picked up the phone as if he might call the police. But he ordered a pizza instead, and when it came, he paid a skinny bearded guy with a sweaty ball of rumpled bills. Then he turned the air conditioning all the way up and ate the pizza wearing just his underpants and the other sock. He moved his sore jaw side to side as he chewed.

When he answered his phone, there was a long silence. "Where are you?" she finally said. Babette's voice was small and sweet, just like when she wanted to talk him into buying Rory a new Xbox or into enrolling him in private school. He wished that he could flip a switch and ignite the passion they used to have, like a gas burner on the GE Deluxe she'd made him replace with that stupid Viking cooktop that they never even used. They'd once stayed in bed for an entire holiday weekend—they'd both lost weight from having sex and not eating.

"I'm at the Battlefield Inn on 29."

"What? Why?"

"I want you to put on something sexy and come out here."

"Dylan's mom picked him up on the shoulder of the highway," she said. "What the hell happened?" Dylan was another gamer who lived out this way. Rory was okay. Thank God. But then also, *Shit*. Rory probably didn't wait five minutes for a lift, probably hadn't given Franz another thought.

"See you soon," he said. "Oh, and bring me some socks." He hung up.

When she arrived, he recognized her particularly loud knock. He let her in, and he took the ball of socks in her hand and threw it over his shoulder.

"Jesus!" she said, when she saw that he was in his underwear.

He reached forward and ripped open her jacket

—or no actually, *Rory*'s jacket. The camouflage one with all the pockets.

"Franz!" she said. She wore a ratty T-shirt and no makeup, and it sure didn't look like those were the outlines of a bustier beneath the cotton. "You left *our son*." Her brow furrowed and she reached out a hand to his cheek. "This is all red." She paused. "I thought he was kidding when he told me he'd hit you."

"It's red from the ice," he said, which wasn't true. He gestured to her clothes. "I mean, the jacket's an interesting touch. But this is it? This is sexy?"

Her face went from concerned to hurt and back to mad in just a few seconds. "Since when do you care about sex? What could be a bigger waste of money than lingerie?" Her eyes glistened with what he thought could be tears, and she wiped her face with the back of her hand. Did Franz want her to cry?

He squeezed his eyes shut for a moment. What he could not stop re-living was that night he picked her up at the police station, after the robbery—the bright red scrape on her forehead that he could see from across the lobby. He'd rushed toward her, arms open, and she had not placed a hand on his chest and said, "I'm good" or "Save it for an episode of *The Waltons*." Instead she'd pressed her bruised face there in the crook of his armpit and hadn't cried or said a word. He'd felt the hot, jagged rhythm of her breath. Maybe if she had cried instead, it wouldn't have been the most terrifying moment of his life.

"Well, why did you even bother with *this*?" he said now, indicating her outfit.

"I was in a hurry, dickhead. I thought maybe you were out here trying to kill yourself."

He wasn't sure exactly why he was frustrated with her—maybe for reacting to him like he was another child to care for, one that she liked a little less than Rory. It hadn't occurred to him she might mistake his agitation for something so dark, so certain —these days his emotional register had shrunk to the point that he envied weeping, scandalized politicians on the news.

Franz took a few steps backward, thinking about what she'd said. "Like Keith Bear," he muttered, sitting on the bed, head in his hands. Keith Bear had been a skinny kid with impossibly tall, teased scarlet hair, a runaway from the Midwest somewhere, and everyone knew him. He'd shot himself in a pay-by-the-hour motel room in 1986.

"Well, what am I supposed to think? The way you've been acting lately."

He patted the bedspread next to him. But she grimaced, continued to pace.

"Rory said you wanted to move," he told her. "To Vegas."

"Don't tell me you believe all of RD's bullshit." She stopped and turned. "The *only* way I'm leaving our new house," she said, "is feet first."

They fell silent then, Franz staring straight ahead at the dusty television and the mini-fridge with the combination lock on it. If he didn't look at the couple in the mirror, or if he squinted at her tiny outline, it was easy to believe they were sixteen, that no time had passed. Way back when, this would have been a dream come true—to have her alone in a hotel room. In his underwear.

He studied her, the straightness of her freckled nose. Jesus, who was he kidding? This was still a dream come true. An army of adolescent boys would have killed to be here with her. Wasn't the problem just that he understood now, in a way he hadn't at sixteen, the complexity, the danger of the human beings inside these bodies? Didn't sex provide glimpses, albeit flickering ones in a woman's gaze, of the needs you *couldn't* satisfy, of the person you weren't?

He forced himself to sit up straighter. Words bubbled in the back of his mouth. And when they came out, his voice sounded unsteady. "What the fuck, little lady. Want to blaze up?" he said, quoting that terrible opening line he'd used so long ago at the Razor Club.

Babette gasped and clapped her hands. "Oh my God," she said, like she'd remembered something. She jumped forward and crouched over the jacket, now in a heap on the floor from where he'd shoved it off her shoulders. She fished something out of the pocket and held it up for his inspection between her thumb and forefinger.

"What's that?"

"It's a joint, dumb ass. What did you think it was?"

"But where did you get it?"

"It was in the jacket."

"I thought that was his 'personal space.'" Franz used Rory's sarcastic finger quotes.

"Shut up," she said, distracted, her eyes lingering on Franz's cheek again.

Franz took the joint, and he got up to study it in the dusty light from the window. There would be a drug test before the new job. This joint would probably ensure he failed it. Albeit with consequences for his career. He found matches on the hotel nightstand. He lit one, held it in front of the joint for a long moment, watched the flame flicker in the gust from the air conditioning. When he finally took a draw, face tilted toward the ceiling, he saw strips of peeling paint. He waved the match to put it out.

"What are you *doing*?" she said.

He let the smoke fill his lungs until they burned, until his chest started to feel like one of those *Firestorm3* mortar shell craters. He stifled a cough as he offered her the joint, and smoke puffed out through his lips.

"Do you want some or not?" he managed to say, sucking the smoke back in.

Babette looked at the joint for a long moment. "Like *that's* what I need," she said, smirking. But then she reached out to take it. She lay back on the bed. She took three sharp, hollow drags and coughed.

Oh, this was good. Better than he remembered. Was this really good shit, or had he just forgotten? He lay down next to her and she passed him the joint. He laughed, the sweet smoke expelling into the room, his shoulders shaking. He wasn't sure what would happen next, if he might start sobbing.

"What's so funny?" she said, turning her head.

He turned his also, so that they were eye to eye. Her breath fluttered his lashes. "Punched his old man, had his weed stolen, probably won a championship," he whispered. "That little shit is having quite a day."

They stared at each other. Her gaze felt good. He didn't know when they had last looked at each other for this long. He fantasized about Babette bringing him a joint every day and smoking it with him during his lunch hour—the way wives in the fifties brought their husbands picnic baskets of fried chicken. Back then, people just didn't talk about their problems.

Maybe this, right now, right here, was all she needed to know. Maybe Texas was rolled up inside this joint, disappearing into the air. He rolled onto his back again and looked at the ceiling. "You're so goddamn hot," he said, resigned, like her hotness was unreasonable.

"Really?" she said, and there was a small, surprised sound in her voice. She'd *never* been one of those women who needed to hear that she was pretty.

"Fuck," he muttered, realizing all over again what they'd lost and the things he'd not understood how to give her.

Babette sighed. "What will we do about Rory?" she said.

He wasn't sure if she meant because of what Rory had done to Franz or because of what Franz had done to Rory or because of what they'd been doing to each other in front of him or because they were both about to be too messed up to drive or what. He closed his eyes. He could see Rory's face on the other side of the glass just before he'd driven away earlier, the intensity of his eyes, like a coyote, a look that he now understood was familiar because it was how Babette used to look. Before.

He opened his own eyes and studied the gold around Babette's pupils, like flames. There was nothing they really *needed* to do about Rory. He felt a pang of sour shame in his stomach. Rory had big brass balls—the kind you needed to change the world. Or no, actually, the kind you needed so the world wouldn't change *you*.

"You mean so he doesn't sell out, like his old man?" said Franz, and he felt his voice waver, as if something might go up in his chest, a landmine, an IED.

She blinked at him, uncomprehending. "What are you talking about, dip wad?" she said, laughing. "I'm the one encouraging our son to play a warmongering video game. And why? To keep myself distracted?" She rubbed her temples with her fingertips. "Look what it's doing to him," she muttered.

Franz reached into the pocket of his pants, draped over a chair, and he pulled out the baggie of bullet casings. "Here's a distraction," he said.

She took the bag, turning it this way and that. She wagged a finger at Franz. "Did you stop these with your chest?" She laughed uncontrollably for a moment. Then she stopped. Her moist eyes blinked at his, and he could see the admiration there—like he really was the hero, someone who took matters into his own hands. He understood then that this was something Babette still believed about him.

He started to wag a finger back at her, and found himself enthralled for a moment by the miraculous way his hands waved in front of him. God he was stoned. "The world doesn't want fucking Superman anymore. His ass would be sued."

Franz reached for his wife and pulled her close, encircling her body with his own.

"Fuck the world," said Babette, gesturing to all that was outside the motel door.

HEAVEN'S DOOR

The Meteorite Man did not need this shit. "For every hour that the grass grows over my rock and *rusts* it . . . " he said to his assistant Hankey, pausing to decide on just the right empty threat, "I'm going to cut off a lock of your hairdo while you're asleep."

Hankey's surfer-dude blond head turned away from the computer screen at a barely perceptible velocity. Hankey blinked, then pulled out one of his ear buds. "Chill," he said. That was it. Just *Chill.* He didn't even make a wisecrack about the Meteorite Man's heart, about the probability of a *third* coronary.

For the tenth time, Hankey played the grainy, three-second footage of the meteorite streaking across the June sky. Then, he clicked the play button again, glancing at the Meteorite Man as if daring him to say something about it.

The Meteorite Man's fingers tingled like he might actually do something—he didn't know what—to Hankey's hair. He stuffed his hands in his pockets and sighed. "You ought to at least flip the coronary card when you're being a dipshit, Junior."

"Zip it, old man."

The Meteorite Man muttered and paced for another minute, and then sidled up behind Hankey's chair, something he knew Hankey didn't like. Hankey hunched forward and lifted his shoulders, as if the Meteorite Man might reach around and twist his nipple. Hankey's fear wasn't unfounded—the Meteorite Man had done this a few times. But now he yanked Hankey's headphone cord out of the computer. Suddenly there was volume.

"There! Turn that up," said the Meteorite Man. "That's the sonic boom. We're within twenty miles of the impact site. I'd put money on it." He clapped his hands and laughed to himself.

"I already know that," muttered Hankey. He plugged the headphones back in, but pulled out the ear buds and let them hang around his neck. "This is exactly why I have to use these. You can't mind your own b-i-d-n-e-s-s." Hankey occasionally spelled out words while bobbing his head like a sassy afternoon talk show host.

Ever since the doctors had implanted that stent, they'd warned the Meteorite Man to retire; he'd told them where they could shove it. But he did agree to hire an assistant and to eat more salads—he'd even made good on the assistant part, which seemed like enough compromise for a lifetime.

"That's good, right? About the sonic boom?" said a voice—it was the amateur astrophotographer, who stood near the sliding glass door on the other side of the room, as if he might slip behind those musty drapes. The Meteorite Man had almost forgotten about him, even though he and Hankey were in the man's apartment. God, this apartment. A divorced man's special—rental unit with walls the color of instant oatmeal. The only decoration was a poster of the Milky Way Galaxy thumb-tacked over a couch that looked like it came from a Motel 6 auction.

"Where are we again?" whispered the Meteorite Man.

"Brilliant," Hankey said in unison with the man across the room, their voices in stereo.

"What—now you're *both* getting fresh with me?"

"No," sighed Hankey. "That's the name of the town. We're in Brilliant."

The Meteorite Man should not have forgotten the name of the goddamn town, even if it was their third or fourth stop through identical backwaters—large white town hall building, brick fire station, four or five churches with imposing steeples, a lap-dancing club called The Palomino or Valentino's or Thumbelina's. This was the first meteorite fall in Maryland since 1923.

He pulled his hands out of his shorts pockets and then wasn't sure what to do with them. They were built for holding cigarettes and whisky. He smiled awkwardly at the man across the room. This guy probably lived out here in bumfuck and commuted over an hour to DC or Baltimore, just so he could see the sky better.

These amateurs—or "amateurites," as the Meteorite Man liked to call them—were all gung ho know-it-alls until something useful actually happened. Then they became stuttering idiots. Still, the man had potentially earned the Meteorite Man his own body weight in gold—something like $800 a gram. The Meteorite Man studied him, really studied him. The guy wasn't bad looking—tall, a full head of salt and pepper hair, chiseled jaw. Three different bicycles hung upside down in the entry way. And he had one honking big-ass telescope on the balcony. Celestron Edge 1400HD. Probably around $10,000. The Meteorite Man experienced a strange little itch that was something like respect.

"So, Chad," the Meteorite Man said, moving across the room, having to reach up to put his arm around those broad shoulders. He maneuvered the man toward the balcony outside the open glass door. "An astrophotographer, huh? And a damn good one. I can see you know your stuff."

"Well," said the amateurite, gesturing to the

telescope, "there really wasn't any skill involved. I programmed her to take five three-minute exposures of Andromeda, and I decided at the last minute to use the video option, too. Then I went in and watched *The Tonight Show*. I was totally bummed when I saw those streaky images. I didn't even know it was a meteorite. If it hadn't been for Mister . . . Mister—Alisso, I think his name was—seeing the photo on my blog—"

"Whoa, whoa. Alisso? Alisso saw these?"

The amateurite nodded. "One of them."

The Meteorite Man looked at Hankey, whose head turned considerably faster this time. Hankey's wide brown eyes—the ones women wrote about in fan letters—searched the Meteorite Man's face, panic in them as if he were a spooked horse. Then Hankey threw his hands in the air and mouthed the words *Jesus fuck me!*

The Meteorite Man motioned calmly toward the floor with his palms, like a preacher easing the congregation into the seats—as if to say *Shhh. I got this.*

"Okay, Chad," said the Meteorite Man, working to keep his voice even. "When was this?"

"You mean when did he comment on my blog or when did he come by?"

"He *came by*?"

"Yeah. About an hour ago."

Out of the corner of his eye, the Meteorite Man saw Hankey drop his head back in response to this news and study the ceiling, but the boy didn't say anything or let out a noisy sigh. He was learning. It was easier to undo a person's allegiance to the competition if you downplayed the stakes.

"And did you show him this video, as well as the photos?" the Meteorite Man continued. He licked a finger and pretended to be interested in a smudge of dirt on his forearm.

"I tried to, but I could hardly get a word in edgewise," said the amateurite, shrugging. The

Meteorite Man studied the guy's face. A word in edgewise? This geek hadn't said boo since they'd arrived, just shown them to the computer and retreated to the door like dumb, happy dog waiting to be walked. "Mr. Alisso looked at the first photo with his 10x Loupe," Chad continued, "and then he took off."

"Ha!" the Meteorite Man clapped his hands. "Classic Alisso!" His rival Alisso's impatience coupled with Chad's reticence had probably saved the hunt, spared the Meteorite Man from making a wasted trip all the way from Arkansas with his goddamn ever-expanding entourage. He patted the amateurite on the back. "It's all good, Chad. It's all good."

Hankey exhaled, shooting the Meteorite Man a relieved look. Then he turned back to the desk, scribbling his calculations in his notepad. The Meteorite Man fought the urge to snatch the pencil out of Hankey's hand. He knew he could calculate faster than anyone, but he didn't allow himself to do the map and compass work anymore, not since he'd had those heart attacks on two different occasions just like this one—when he'd been figuring a zero-degree line between a camera and a strewn field. He'd chosen Hankey—who was good—who'd been breathing down the Meteorite Man's neck every time he went on a hunt in Texas. But who was also only twenty-six years old. Look at him there in those baggy shorts and the muscle shirt and barely able to grow that scraggly goatee beard. A kid. The Meteorite Man did have to admit, though, that he had earned more disposable income since Hankey had been featured on the show. And the chicks. Man, the chicks! Somehow, the Meteorite Man's sex appeal multiplied exponentially with the addition of a sidekick. It made him wish he still cared about getting laid by twenty-something groupies. The universe did have a sense of humor.

That reminded him—goddamn Lenny out in the hallway. He'd be pissed, yet again, that the Meteorite

Man had not let them start filming. It was Lenny's own stupid fault for bringing a new camera man. How could the Meteorite Man be sure the guy wasn't Alisso's mole? Alisso wasn't just liberal with bribes; he wasn't just charming. When charm didn't work, he could be ruthless; he had a way of getting people into his pocket one way or the other.

The Meteorite Man said, "Listen, Chad, no one else has been here, right? Not Schaffer? Or Donnelly?"

Chad shook his head.

"Okay, good. I'll tell you what. You pretend the rest of those guys—especially Alisso—they don't exist. These pictures, and this video—they belong to the Meteorite Man now. You do that for me, and you can come with us tonight on the hunt."

He thought about promising Chad a cut of the profits or a role on this episode of the show, but one thing the Meteorite Man had learned over the years was that amateurites didn't care much about money or even fame. They were mostly would-be astronauts whose asthma or overbearing mothers had dashed their dreams of space. Which suited the Meteorite Man fine.

There was no way he was letting Chad Barkley out of his sight—it would be like the frigging witness protection program—or no, the Alisso Protection Program. That unscrupulous fuck was so out of control, it was a wonder he hadn't taken to murdering the Chad Barkleys of the world just to cover his tracks. The Meteorite Man had once untied a retired carnival worker and his wife who he'd found in a closet of their own home after one of Alisso's visits. He'd found a note taped to the man's chest: *Too slow, Chester.* The Meteorite Man's name was not *Chester*, but that's the sort of character Alisso was—someone who sought to demean you by calling you *Chester* or *Skippy* or *Chucky.*

The Meteorite Man would never understand why his own ex-wife, Marianne, had fallen for Alisso. It shouldn't have mattered that the three of them went way back. She could have done so much better. She had been single for two years after their divorce and was so pretty—with wavy dark brown hair, a tiny waist, and feet you wanted to put in your mouth —who wouldn't have wanted her? Alisso had been with Marianne for three years now. The Meteorite Man pictured her kissing Alisso's thin, chapped lips and shuddered. It must be about power. Alisso made women think that he had it. It was sleight of hand, his Houdini-like ability to flim-flam so many, that had gotten him this far.

"All right," said Hankey, standing up from Chad's computer desk. "Let's go to the water treatment plant."

"You sure?" said the Meteorite Man. Hankey had screwed up their last gig by putting the decimal point in the wrong place when he triangulated the possible impact zone. They had ended up at a Jack in the Box outside Houston while Alisso got the prize, forty miles away in El Cielo del Campo. It wasn't bad enough that half his money went to Marianne, and therefore by default to Alisso (the wise bastard was a live-in boyfriend, not Marianne's second husband). But now, now Alisso also had one of the rare pieces of lunar rock from this decade, something which rightfully should have belonged to the Meteorite Man, which would have belonged to him, no question, ten years earlier. Before he needed goddamn Hankey, who would have been *sixteen* at the time.

"Yes," said Hankey, hands raised defensively. "I'm sure. I'm fucking positive."

If that sonic boom happened when the amateurite's video suggested it did—Shazam! They were in the less-than-twenty-four-hour money. Not only that, but witnessed falls increased the value of meteorites exponentially. This one had not only been seen by at least 100 people, but had also been caught on numerous cameras, including the one at the water treatment plant. And the size of the thing! It would make El Cielo del Campo look like a rusted, lonesome pebble.

"Because this is a big one," said the Meteorite Man. "It could be *the* big one."

"Yeah, no shit," said Hankey. Then he seemed to grit his teeth and swallow a curse, which unsettled the Meteorite Man because Hankey didn't usually hold back.

"Fine, it's cool," said the Meteorite Man. "Keep your muscle shirt on."

Hankey gathered his equipment into his Billabong backpack. Billabong had become one of the show's sponsors since Hankey had gotten on camera, and now Lenny was always finding excuses to film right behind the backpack as they walked. It irked the Meteorite Man a little.

"At least I can *wear* a muscle shirt," Hankey said.

Ah, that was more like it. The Meteorite Man smiled the smile he knew Hankey hated, then he held —up to his forehead—three fingers in the shape of a *W*. "Whatever, Pretty Boy." He made a muscle and slapped it with his other hand. It might have been true that his diet was terrible—his favorite meal was the Bacon Cheddar Melt at Arby's—but he was still lean and wiry for a fifty-nine-year-old legend. "Like iron, kid."

Hankey rolled his eyes. "More like chrondite. And just as old."

"Come on, Barkley," said the Meteorite Man to Chad. "It's show time."

Out in the hall, Lenny and the crew walked backward, filming as the Meteorite Man summed up what they had found in the amateurite's apartment.

"Cut. Good, good," said Lenny. Then to the amatuerite: "You can give us your video?"

"Sure, you bet," said Chad. He had the wondering eyes of a puppy taking his first steps on grass. Just how the Meteorite Man wanted him.

"Oh, man, Lenny." He turned to the camera man as they approached the elevator. "You smell like the fucking perfume counter at Bloomingdale's."

Hankey laughed out loud, then gave the Meteorite Man a fist bump. "I didn't want to say it."

"What?" Lenny looked hurt. "This is Axe. It's body wash."

"It's douche," said the Meteorite Man. "For douche bags."

All the guys in the crew cracked up, but not the Meteorite Man. He studied Lenny's face. Lenny with his art school glasses and sarcastic T-shirts. Jesus. These producers. Did they actually think TV was art? What they did was as rigid and formulaic as an auto assembly line, which was where the Meteorite Man's father had worked. His father had dropped dead at the plant when he was two years younger than the Meteorite Man was now.

Out in the parking lot, the Meteorite Man studied the sky—a few cumulus clouds across the pinkening dusk, nothing to worry about yet, though rain was due from the south tomorrow morning. The winds that would bring it had already whipped up, and the Meteorite Man could feel the hair on his legs. "Hold still," he said to Hankey. He reached into the side pocket of the younger man's backpack to retrieve the detachable legs from his cargo pants, which he now zipped back onto the bottom of his shorts. While he had the backpack open, he pretended to fish his beta blocker from the bottle and then pretended to swallow it for the benefit of Hankey and Lenny, who harassed him daily to take his meds. The betas made him sluggish and surely he could skip one just this once. If they didn't find the meteorite before 24 hours went by, its value would plummet. And if it rained, and the thing rusted? "Gear up, everyone. It's going to be a long night." He stood up and surveyed the lot. Then he said to Lenny: "Keep that monstrosity of a van away from my car."

"We'll be invisible," said Lenny, which the Meteorite Man knew wasn't true.

"If Alisso spots us," the Meteorite Man continued, "I'm selling that camera on eBay so I can make alimony."

Just six months ago, he had persuaded Lenny to stop driving that van that said *The Air and Space Channel* on the side of it. Still, a huge white conversion van was anything but inconspicuous. The Meteorite Man himself always used a rental, and always a different make and model each time.

Meteorite Man looked up and down the parking lot for cars that might be surveilling them. So far so good.

At the water treatment plant, Hankey sweet-talked the foreman into letting them watch the closed circuit TV tapes from the night before. That was another thing Hankey did better—he played the dopey surfer dude to a tee, and he always pointed out the TV camera waiting outside. Turned out every schmo in the USA would risk his job and his kids' futures to have his face on the tube for five seconds. The Meteorite Man understood. He used to give two shits about being on TV, the attention it brought, the attention he *thought* he wanted. He liked the money; he liked the legitimacy; and he *loved* being able to lord it over Alisso. But as for possessing a face people recognized—was that really an accomplishment? Goddamn Colonel Sanders had that.

When they piled into the cramped booth to watch the tape, the Meteorite Man fought the urge to elbow Lenny, who leaned into him, pressed by the crew, the camera, and the boom. It was hard to breathe. Meteorite Man was sweating, and regretted zipping those pant legs back on. The security guard pressed play, and then the Meteorite Man gasped. The footage was not black and white or grainy; it was as sharp and colorful and clear as the high definition television he had at home.

"Whoa!" said Hankey.

The crew echoed him: "Whoa!"

"Damn, that's good quality," someone said. "Who funds this crib, a drug lord?"

They had to watch a half an hour's worth of footage, waiting for that one second when the meteorite would streak across darkening sky on the screen. And they couldn't afford to blink. Fifteen minutes went by, and then another ten minutes that felt like an hour. The Meteorite Man kept wiping his face, but his hand was wet and it didn't do any good. He was probably addicted to those damned beta blockers.

"Oh my God! There it is," said the amateurite.

"We got it," said Hankey.

The Meteorite Man had been studying the moisture on his fingertips and missed the whole thing. When he looked up, the amateurite was still pointing at the screen, where there remained a greenish glow. "Let's see it again," he said.

The security guard hit the rewind button, and he played it again, this time in slow motion. The Meteorite Man opened his eyes wide and willed himself not to blink. But this was not the dingy gray flash he'd seen so many times before on closed circuit TVs all over Texas and Arkansas. Instead, a colorful fireball burst across the giant screen, breaking up as it fell, sparkling like a firework. The light illuminated the faces of the open-mouthed crew. "Damn," muttered Hankey. A trail remained for a full minute, sinuous and smoky against the purple twilight, a slight bend in it. In his whole career, the Meteorite Man had not come this close to witnessing a fall for himself. The only time he'd seen one with his own eyes had been the time that started it all, the time when he was twelve and he'd been standing outside the funeral home in Lutherville, Texas, his father's hometown.

"What are you doing out here, young man?" said his mother when she found him sitting on the back steps, chin in his hands.

"We don't know any of these people. How can we leave him here?"

She had shrugged. "This is where his family is buried."

"*We're* his family."

"They were his family longer." His father had been twenty years older than his mother, embarking on this second marriage at forty-three.

She kissed her hand and pressed it to his cheek before she got up and went back inside. It was the last time she'd made that particular gesture—certainly she never did it anymore after she married Larry, the shoe salesman, back in Arkansas and began to produce those four more kids.

When he'd stood up to go back inside, he'd stuffed his hands in the pockets of his new stiff dress pants and he'd sighed and tilted his face toward the sky, and that was when he'd seen it. Like this footage on the screen—the sparkle across the purple dusk. He had almost forgotten how bright it had been, almost like it was alive.

"Did you get it?" said Lenny now.

"Yup," said Zane, the camera man.

"Perfect," said the Meteorite Man, wondering if anyone had noticed how pallid he must look. He'd suddenly gone from sweltering to shivering, just as he had shivered that night in his twelve-year-old body, as if the fiery sparkle in the sky were now tingling inside his kneecaps, his stomach, his fingertips. He brought his elbow to his face now and wiped it good, and then he tried to stand taller. Hankey sidled in close and showed him some numbers he had scribbled on his clipboard. They locked eyes. "Ten miles northeast," they both said. The Meteorite Man laughed and patted Hankey on the back. Outside the booth, he drew several deep breaths. "Every hunt could be your last," he muttered to himself, quoting something his doctor had said at a recent check up.

It was then that the Meteorite Man glanced over

and noticed the amateurite had tears in his eyes. *Oh Christ.* He patted Barkley on the back, too. "This is getting good, Chad. With any luck, you'll make history tonight."

"This is so cool," said Barkley, dabbing at his eyes with the *Meteorite Man* terrycloth wristband that someone from the crew had given him.

Lenny put his hand on the Meteorite Man's shoulder on the way out to the car and leaned in close. "This is why you have the highest ratings on the Air and Space Channel."

"This isn't about ratings," said the Meteorite Man. He shrugged off Lenny's hand.

By the time they'd driven ten miles to Catonsville, a hamlet just outside Baltimore, it was 7 p.m. They had the advantage over Alisso because the TV crew gave them credibility as they slogged door-to-door. They weren't just a couple of creepy guys trying to gain access to the backyard. In fact, when he and the crew showed up, housewives squealed and said, "My hair looks a mess!"

By 9 p.m., they'd canvassed nearly half the town, or at least it felt like it. "Could we have miscalculated?" the Meteorite Man said to Hankey. His right knee hurt, as it sometimes did before a storm.

Hankey stopped walking and turned to face the Meteorite Man: "We did *not* miscalculate. It's here. We just have to be the ones stubborn enough to find it." Then he gasped with exasperation: "You're the one who taught me that, dickhead!"

With that, Hankey marched off toward the next house. Damn it, he was right. The Meteorite Man had seen all the calculations for himself. What the hell was his problem?

Just then a woman in running clothes huffed past the Meteorite Man and grabbed Hankey's arm. The Meteorite Man recognized her from one of the first houses they'd visited a few hours ago—large Rottweiler, no husband in sight, tight juicy ass. "I just got off the phone with my friend Abilene. She lives over there." The blonde pointed to the next block, one they hadn't done yet. "I forgot until you left—she said something hit her roof last night. She thought maybe it had been a really aggressive squirrel throwing rocks from a tree or something."

The Meteorite Man and the amateurite took off running, Hankey and the hot blonde close behind. Count on Hankey to score every time. The kid was an asset.

"Wait!" Lenny called. "We can't go that fast!"

When they got to the house, the hot blonde's friend already stood there with the front door open, silhouetted against the warm light from inside. When they got closer, they saw a giant redhead in a tight blue dress. Or no, actually, as they got closer still, they saw a man in a tight blue dress and barefoot. The Meteorite Man laughed out loud. Excellent! Now Lenny could stop worrying about the episode, about what its hook would be. He would interview Miss Information, and leave the Meteorite Man alone. Hallelujah. The Meteorite Man hugged her in greeting and then gave her a big kiss on the cheek.

"Well hello yourself," she said, blushing, one hand fluttering over her chest. "Come right in. Go right up to the attic."

She followed them, jabbering about the racket the night before.

"What time was that?" said Hankey.

"What time did I call you, Sugar?" she said to the hot blonde, who didn't seem to know the answer. They looked at each other quizzically for a moment. "Mmmm . . . . Maybe nine?"

She then paused at the door to the attic, and flipped on the light in the stairwell. The Meteorite Man and Hankey had already begun to traipse up the steps, and suddenly saw ahead the illuminated wooden eaves of the low attic ceiling. Below, the amateurite was saying, "After you, Ma'am."

When Lenny and Zane got to the top of the steps, they shined the powerful spotlight from the camera. And zow! There it was resting on top of a box marked *Football trophies*—a two or three gram dull black nugget with the characteristic thumbprints, the regmaglypts. Hankey picked it up and held in front of the Meteorite Man's eyes for inspection. There were visible streamlines from the entry into Earth's atmosphere, so there wasn't even any point in wasting time with the diamond file and digging beneath the fusion crust to double check that it wasn't just a rock. Jesus, the Meteorite Man's whole scalp began to tingle like it might lift off and crawl down his face like a centipede—a feeling he hadn't had in a long time. He and Hankey both shoved some boxes out of the way and examined the hole in the roof. Even though the hole was only about two inches in diameter, the wind whistled into it, and he could see the alarmingly fast movement of the clouds two miles up. The fragment had entered from a southeasterly direction. "I bet I can guess where the big boy is," said the Meteorite Man, longitude lines triangulating in his head.

"Me, too," said Hankey. The two of them looked at one another for a moment and then turned back the way they had come, shoving past Lenny, the crew, Miss Information, the hot blonde, and the amateurite, all clustered at the top of the steps like people who'd gotten lost in a mall.

The two of them hot-footed their way back down the stairs, fast as tap dancers, giggling all the while. Hankey moved faster, and the Meteorite Man tried to slow him by grabbing his backpack. The amateurite had regained his senses, and clomped down the stairs behind them.

When the three of them, in the rental, reached the approximate spot, a half mile to the northwest, they found themselves at Francis Scott Key Middle School. The van hadn't caught up yet, but wouldn't be far behind.

Just then, a red car swerved past them, tires screeching, and halted right in front, perpendicular to them like a police car ending a high speed chase. Alisso. He clambered out of the driver's seat and trotted toward them, leaving his door wide open. Then he was rapping on the Meteorite's window. He said: "You're too late, Sparky. Check out this shit." He held up a fist-sized meteorite, worth probably $5,000.

The Meteorite Man did his best to make a pissed off face. Then he turned to Hankey and exclaimed, "Damn it to hell!"

Alisso hadn't seen the video or heard the boom, so he had no idea that the rock in his hand was not the big boy. It was all the Meteorite Man could do to keep himself from giggling again. He dared not look at Hankey.

As the two of them trudged into the knee-high grass behind the school, Alisso shouted, "All you're going to find out there is scrabble." The Meteorite Man glanced over his shoulder and watched Alisso cup his hand up to his mouth so he could project better. "This guy," he called, kissing the rock with a loud smack, "was two miles from here. You're nowhere close!"

The Meteorite Man flipped Alisso the bird and heard Alisso bray his donkey laugh. Somewhere behind them in the darkness, Lenny had arrived, and the Meteorite Man could hear the voices of the hot blonde and Miss Information, too.

Lenny—leading the camera and the sound boom through the tall grass—had obviously clocked Alisso's rock because he was saying, "Fuck, fuck, fuck," under his breath. Normally Lenny never cursed, as he'd be the one to have to edit it out later.

Barkley, who'd done the polite thing and waited for Lenny, now ran to catch up, his face ashen in the bright light from Zane's camera, which shone out onto the field. "I'm so sorry," he said. "I feel like this is all my fault."

"Eyes down, Barkley," said the Meteorite Man gently. "Look for something dark and knobby."

If he craned his head around Barkley's tree-like frame, he could see in the distance the silhouette of Alisso eating a Quiznos sub on the hood of the Meteorite Man's rental car, the wrapper flapping in the wind so that he had to keep pulling it out of his mouth. There would be mustard and mayonnaise smeared on the paint job. He would leave his trash on the Meteorite Man's seat. It was how Alisso liked to celebrate his wins whenever he got the chance. His bald head shone under the streetlight, and he was jabbering away on the phone as he ate, undoubtedly to Marianne. The Meteorite Man hated to admit to himself how comforting this was—the predictability of Alisso and also the fact that Marianne was still tied to his life, albeit indirectly.

The wind carried Alisso's weedy voice. "I'm taking you to Vegas," he was saying now. "Okay, well then, someplace else. Tell me where you want to go." It had never occurred to the Meteorite Man to take Marianne anywhere when they were married. He'd hardly ever gone home between hunts—unlike Alisso. It was nice to think that she had that now, that she wasn't lonely like before.

The streetlight way out in front of the school, beyond where Alisso lounged, cast his rival in backlit shadow. The faint warm light delineated the dark outline of his body, charted the wide arc of his beer belly. The Meteorite Man experienced a kind of double vision—he could see Alisso as he was now and also as he'd been at Hankey's age. Long hair in a ponytail, a baby face that wouldn't grow a beard. Still chubby, of course, but less so—wide across the chest instead of across the midsection. They'd both been interns for Quentin McCarthy, the best meteorite hunter of his day, before the advent of the big magnets. The Meteorite Man had played second fiddle to Alisso for the better part of a year, supplying calculations and priming Quentin McCarthy's gear while Alisso trotted out front like an overfed hunting dog and retrieved the prizes.

Alisso had been there in the office when the Meteorite Man had first asked out Marianne, McCarthy's indispensible administrative assistant. "You bastard," Alisso had said later, in the lab. "You knew I was going to ask her." His baby face, those large brown eyes, looked shocked, as if the Meteorite Man had refused to carry the crew's gear as he normally did or had failed to relinquish the last sandwich and go hungry. In fact, the Meteorite Man had *not* known about Alisso's designs on Marianne, but he did know one thing. Alisso's jealousy, the way the Meteorite Man suddenly mattered, had been exhilarating—almost as good as the first time he'd held that meteorite fragment in his hand when he was twelve, a fragment he'd made his mother take him to see the following night on a display table outside the fire station. Closing his fingers tightly around it, stretching his arm toward the sky as if his fist were the moon, it had been as if the knobby chunk of iron might awaken like a rocket to propel itself home, as if it might take him with it.

Now, the glee was like a pain in the Meteorite Man's ribcage. A light feeling—the opposite of heart attack pain—like he could fly.

Hankey had trudged ahead off to the right with his own flashlight and the magnetic wand, which resembled a walking stick. The amateurite shadowed Hankey, pointing at chunks of asphalt nestled in the grass, saying, "What's that?" If you didn't know, you'd think the two of them were a couple searching for seashells on a beach.

"Stop," shouted Hankey at Barkley, struggling to be heard over the wind. "When we see it, I'll tell you."

The Meteorite Man paused then to straighten his back, stretching to one side and the other, hands on his hips. He massaged his neck, studying the clouds which had become cumulonimbus, had sunk lower in the sky. He turned his head as far as he could one way and then the other, trying to make his vertebrae pop.

It was then that his eyes fixed on the abandoned school bus farther out in the weeds. And they registered the completely shattered windshield, fresh glass on the snub-nosed yellow hood. But he did not shout out, as he imagined he would. He did not crow.

A meteorite of that size. One that had landed within the shelter of a bus instead of on the ground. Well, its value was beyond even his own calculations. But he did not speak. The light feeling inside his chest swelled like helium against his breastbone, and it felt like hope—the hope that if he stood very still, if he did not yet go over and tap Lenny's shoulder and quietly wave him toward the bus, the earth would cease its relentless rotation. Nothing would change. Not a single thing.

He turned and surveyed his own immediate horizon—Alisso lying back on the hood of the car, hands clasped behind his head; Miss Information and the hot blonde picking arm in arm through the grass with their own flashlight, hair flying every which way; Hankey and Barkley hunching forward against the wind at the same angle as the meteorite had flown through the June sky; Lenny and Zane and the crew making themselves as motionless and quiet as the air had been the night before, the night it landed.

Probably if you'd been standing in this field, you would have heard the sonic boom, like a boulder pounding on the sky's door, and half a minute later you would have heard the rock's first experience of air, the sound of friction, that whooshing overhead, above the fireflies, and then finally the crash through the bus glass. But if the Meteorite Man could choose between being here last night to witness that miracle of the heavens or being here tonight—he'd choose this moment, this miracle, right now. His twenty-four hours were almost up.

ABOUT THE AUTHOR

Kathy Flann's fiction has appeared in *Shenandoah*, *The North American Review*, *The Michigan Quarterly Review*, *New Stories from the South*, and other publications. A previous short story collection, *Smoky Ordinary*, won the Serena McDonald Kennedy Award and was published by Snake Nation Press. A novella entitled *Mad Dog* won the AE Coppard Award at White Eagle Coffee Store Press. Flann has an MFA from UNC-Greensboro, and she served as fiction editor of *The Greensboro Review*. For five years, she taught creative writing at the University of Cumbria in England, where she created mini-courses for the BBC's *Get Writing* website and served on the board of the National Association of Writers in Education. Her column, "Letter from America," appears in a UK magazine called *Writing in Education*. She has been a fellow at the Virginia Center for the Creative Arts, Le Moulin à Nef in France, and the Sozopol Fiction Seminars in Bulgaria. She teaches creative writing at Goucher College in Baltimore, Maryland, where she lives with her husband, Howard.